CHUPACARTER

CHUPACARTER

GEORGE LOPEZ

WITH
RYAN CALEJO

ILLUSTRATED BY
SANTY GUTIÉRREZ

VIKING

VIKING

An imprint of Penguin Random House LLC, New York

First published in the United States of America by Viking,
an imprint of Penguin Random House LLC, 2022

Visit us online at penguinrandomhouse.com.

Library of Congress Cataloging-in-Publication Data is available.

Printed in the United States of America

ISBN 9780593465974

1st Printing

LSCH

Design by Opal Roengchai
Text set in Athelas

To the moon—thank you

—G. L.

To our abuelitas

—R. C.

To my beloved family and friends,

and to those who share our culture

here and beyond the ocean

—S. G.

CHUPA

(*choo*-pah)
verb: to slurp or drink greedily

CABRA

(*kah*-brah)
noun: a goat

CHAPTER 1

"Georgie!"

I didn't answer.

"¡Georgie! ¡Bájate ya!"

A chancla went whistling over my head to clunk off the rooster-shaped weather vane above the chimney.

I still didn't answer.

She could throw all the sandals she wanted. I wasn't coming down.

"*Jorge. Eduardo. ¡Lopez! ¡Voy a contar hasta diez!*"

There was a loud *clang, clang, clang!* as my grandma began banging her broom along the edge of the roof like she was trying to scare down a stray cat or something.

I wasn't a cat. That wasn't going to work, either.

Lying back, I tried to make myself comfy. Problem was, my abuela's roof *stunk*. It was one of those tar-and-shingle jobs with nails sticking out all over the place and that awful layer of grainy, gritty sand that scraped and scratched and got stuck in the skin of your hands and knees.

My roof back home was waaay better. The Spanish tiles were all nice and smooth and felt almost like glass against your back. I could lie out on those all night, if I really wanted to. And I had, a couple of times.

"Jorge, do *not* make me climb up there, ¿me oíste?"

A big ole rock came whizzing up out of the dark. No, not a rock. It was one of my grandma's *empanadas*!

I ducked as it thudded off the side of the chimney, leaving a golf-ball-size greasy spot on the old bricks.

"Yeah, malcriado, *seriously*! You want to stay up there? *Fine*. But you *are* going to eat!" And she lobbed another empanada.

This one sailed high over the roof and bounced to a stop right between my sneakers.

I sighed.

I honestly couldn't believe my life right now.

Here I was, stuck in the middle of some giant dust bowl with my abuela chucking deep-fried Mexican pastries at me.

I mean, could it *get* any worse?

"Lemme know if you want some refried beans with that!" Paz yelled from below.

My grandma's full name was Benita de la Paz Campos Sofia Andrea de la Rocha Lopez. Everyone mostly just called her Paz, though, which was sort of ironic because in Spanish, "paz" means *peace* and there really wasn't anything awfully peaceful about my sweet old granny.

My abuela might've had all the dimensions of a hobbit, but she was as strong as an ox—and probably as stubborn as one, too.

In fact, not even my mom liked to argue with her, and my mom was basically the world heavyweight *champ* of arguing. Which told you pretty much everything you needed to know about Señorita Paz.

A split second later, I heard this low whispery hiss, and something arced over the edge of the roof, silvery-white against the pitch-dark sky.

Then that something came crashing down behind me with a loud *SPLASH!*

Suddenly, little rivers of freezing cold water were racing down the shingles, soaking my shorts, my socks—*everything*—and I was just trying to scoot out of the way!

Grandma, FOR REAL?

SPLOOSH

I mean, the lady had turned la manguera on me! Yeah. The flipping *garden hose!*

"Hey, you asked me if it ever rained in this place … Well, *wacha*, it's raining now!"

"Grandma, I *told* you already! I climb up on the roof all the time at my house! Now, can you *please* leave me alone?"

"¿Qué I-do-this-all-the-time, ni I-do-this-all-the-time? ¿Estás loco? Óyeme, your ten seconds are up. Which means *I'm* coming up!"

From down below came the squeal of the porch door opening and closing on rusty hinges.

"Déjalo *ya*, Paz … por Dios."

That was my grandpa. His name is Patricio, and if my abuela was fire, that dude was an arctic glacier.

"He's a big boy," said Patricio. "He found his way up, he'll find his way back down—it's gravity."

"A *big boy*?" snapped my grandma. "The only thing *big* on that one is *his head!*"

I watched their shadows stretch long and dark in the flickering porch light as they argued back and forth, and back and forth, until finally my grandma handed my grandpa the hissing garden hose and then stomped off on her remaining chancla.

"Thank you!" I shouted as they both disappeared back inside. Still arguing, of course.

Then I spent the next five minutes just sort of staring around at the acres and acres of dusty—well, *nothingness*.

Seriously.

There was nothing to see.

You couldn't even hear anything. No cars. No radios. No buses passing by. "Ni un pedo," as my abuela liked to say.

Someone could die of boredom out here. They really could.

Supposedly, though, like a zillion years ago when my grandparents were little, this place had been a beautiful farm. Fifty square acres of Angelonia plants and fruit trees and all that kind of stuff.

My great-great-grandparents had grown apples here, they'd planted gardens here, they'd even raised goats here. I knew this because my mom hadn't stopped yapping about it for, like, two straight weeks. She'd even shown me pictures. Then, when she felt me nibbling at the cheese, she'd sprung her trap.

"You're going to be living with your grandparents for a little while, okay, baby? They're super nice. You're going to have a great time, okay, baby?"

That's how you could tell my mom was feeling desperate. When she started with the whole "okay, baby?" stuff.

Anyway, no amount of whining or arguing or tantrum-throwing or even *begging* had changed her mind. Not even when I'd tried to explain, very calmly, that people just didn't *do* this. No one leaves California—especially not Los Angeles—to move to some dusty, deserted, desert-y armpit of a town in the middle of Nowheresville, New Mexico.

"Remember, you brought this on yourself, okay, baby?"

That had been her big comeback. As if this was all *my* fault or something.

And okay, I'll admit it. I wasn't exactly making my mom's life any easier lately. Like last month, when this big burro of a bully in my math class broke my pencil for probably the *millionth* time, I tried to teach him a physics lesson in trajectory with a spitwad and a paper straw.

I hadn't been *aiming* for Mrs. Jiménez, but of course *I* got detention. And a couple days later, when the same overgrown dill weed had made some racist remark about me going back to my own country, as if America *wasn't* my home, as if I hadn't been born here—just the same as him—I might've said some not-so-nice things, and maybe done some other not-so-nice stuff, too. (On a side note, people who judge others by the color of their skin or the language they grew up speaking really get on my nerves. But I'm not trying to make excuses for what I did. "Two wrongs don't make a right" and all that.)

Where was I?

Ah. Right. Me getting kicked out of school.

Yeah, so after that whole fiasco, Mom pretty much broke down. She went into this huge speech about how I was making all these problems for her and how she couldn't "handle" me anymore and blah, blah, blah.

I knew the truth, though. My mom had a lot of problems right now. I just happened to be the one she could dump on someone else.

For the record, I'm not a bad kid or anything. I'm not some *angel*. I'm not saying that. But it's not like I run around setting things on fire and kicking cats.

I have a smart mouth. That's my "fatal flaw," according to Mr. Mateo, the vice principal at my old school.

"Your smart mouth just bought you a one-way ticket to detention," he'd say. Or "Your smart mouth has officially earned you a coveted spot on cafeteria cleanup duty." He was always saying corny stuff like that. Which I thought was kind of hilarious, because wasn't that the whole point of school? To make you smart? What a menso . . .

Far away, the wind whispered in the dark and then a sudden gust blew in bits of rocks and sticks and spun good ole Señor Rooster, making him wobble and squeak.

It was nothing like the wind back home. It smelled dry and dead and completely unfamiliar.

Man, I was going to miss L.A. In fact, I'd only been away two measly days, and I was already missing it!

And the worst part? My mom hadn't even said how long I'd be stuck out here. I mean, a weekend? Sure. A week? *Fine.* I could probably live with a week.

But all she'd said was, and I quote, "Until I get some things straightened out." Yeah, well, when was that going to be? Next month? Next year? Next *ice age*?

Ugh. Groaning, I glared around at the stupid fields and the stupid hills and all the acres and acres of stupid dirt that didn't really grow anything anymore, except for weeds and some thorny bushes.

All the land, for as far as I could see, was dark and silent; but overhead the moon was bright blue and screaming. It was bigger out here in the middle of nowhere. Brighter, too. But it was still the same moon. Same as yesterday, same as tomorrow.

And it always found me.

The moon was the reason I liked climbing up on roofs at night. Sometimes I felt like it was up there just for me. Shining just so I could see it.

It was the only thing in my life that had never ditched me. And right now it was the *only* thing holding back my tears.

I locked my arms around my knees, hating life right now. Hating *everything* right now. The truth was, I missed my mom, and I missed *my* roof. I missed my room, and our little town house near the river, and the pizza place down the street, and the comic book store at the corner that always had my favorite sketching pads on sale.

I even missed Ernesto's, which was this tiny Puerto Rican restaurant where I helped out about once a week. I wasn't *technically* allowed to work there, but the owner was this pretty cool lady who knew that my mom sometimes struggled with the rent, so she'd pay me a little to help out. Y'know, carry boxes around, straighten tables, that kind of thing.

It wasn't fun or anything, but Mom and I had pretty much been on our own since my dad ran out on us, so we did what we had to do.

I don't think my mom ever knew where the extra money came from. But I'd even managed to save up enough for a new baseball mitt.

Oh, man, baseball . . .

I didn't even want to *think* about baseball!

I'd left my entire Little League team back in L.A. . . . . All my friends. *Everybody.* I mean, who was I supposed to practice with now?

I could practically feel the steam pouring out of my ears, teakettle style, as I snatched up the closest empanada and slung it sidearm into the night. It flew low and straight, kind of like a baseball—geez, there

I go again—and went crashing through the branches of a big pine tree.

Other than the little lemon tree by the garage (which had been my citrus-scented ladder up here), that pine was the only thing growing within probably fifty acres. It stood at the opposite end of the house, a crooked wooden finger pointing up at the stars.

Anyway, I'd been aiming for its trunk, and since I had a pretty good arm (and since my abuela's deep-frying technique apparently turned dough into concrete), I'd been expecting to hear a nice satisfying *clunk!*

So you can imagine my surprise when what I heard instead was "*Ow!*"

Like, *Ouch!*

Like, someone getting hit in the head by a rock. Or in this case, a rock-hard pastry.

Then it hit *me*—

Oh, snap, somebody is in that tree!

CHAPTER 2

For a heart-stopping second, I thought it was my abuela—was *positive*, in fact—and, in my panic, I nearly shrieked, "Grandma, stop playing! I'm getting down, okay?"

But then I realized that there was no way she could've climbed that tree. *I* couldn't even climb that tree. There weren't enough low branches.

"Hey! Who—who's there?" I shouted, jumping to my feet.

But for several seconds there was only silence (well, that and the wild *blam-blam-blam* of my suddenly racing corazón).

Backing slowly away, I yelled, "I know you're in there, dude! I *heard* you!"

Still no answer. Just the sound of the wind

whistling in the little lemon tree and in the pine and in the eaves of the old roof.

"If you don't answer, I'm going to scream!" I warned. "And you do *not* want my grandma to come out here, bro. She's got a broom and she ain't afraid to use it!"

The threat worked.

"Oh, I'll scream!" I said. "You try anything and that's *exactly* what I'm going to do! I'm a screamer. Loudest you ever heard!" I paused. "Hey, how come I can't see you?"

A short silence.

"'Cause I'm hidin'," answered the voice (real smart-alecky, too).

"Yeah, that I *can* see. You plan on coming out?"

"Not really."

Of course not, I thought. *Dude's probably a criminal or something. I bet he just robbed the local 7-Eleven and is hiding up in my abuela's tree! Only—*

—only he didn't *sound* like a criminal.

He sounded more like . . . a *kid.*

Probably twelve like me. Or even a little younger. Ten or eleven, maybe.

"Dude, what the heck are you doing in there?" I said, scooting a little closer to the pine.

"Te dije—I'm hidin'."

"Hiding from *what*? The moon?" I mean, let's be real—there probably wasn't another living soul for a gazillion miles!

He answered, "Una tormenta's comin'," and that's when I noticed the strange way he spoke. Sort of dragging his s's a bit, like he was trying to push the words past a mouthful of braces or something.

"Bro, what are you talking about?" I said. "I don't see any storm." In fact, the sky was almost completely clear; just a few wispy grayish clouds way out there on the hazy horizon.

"You can't smell it? It's gonna be *bad*."

I sniffed at the air a couple of times, but all I smelled was dirt. Which, by the way, was what everything around here smelled like.

Squinting into the branches, I said, "Hey, so you hang out in trees a lot?"

"Sometimes. You hang out on techos a lot?"

Ha. Touché. "Yeah, sometimes."

Silence.

"You speak Spanish, huh?" I said.

"It was my first language. You?"

"Yeah. It was my first language, too." I blinked, still squinting into the shadowy branches. The guy was practically invisible in there. *Must be a pretty tiny chamaco*, I thought. "What's, uh—what's your name, dude?"

"Carter."

"Cool. I'm Jorge."

"I know. I heard your abuelita."

Yeah, I bet he had. People on the other side of the country had probably heard her. "You, um, live around here?"

"Kinda."

"Like, *close*?"

"Kinda."

"You go to school around here?"

"Kinda."

Dodge questions much? I thought.

Then it all finally clicked.

"Bro," I whispered, "are you, like—*running away from home or something*?"

There was a pause. A pretty long one, too. Which was all I needed to hear.

At last the voice said, "Kinda."

He sounded even younger now. And sad. And scared. And all alone. And honestly, I started to feel sort of sorry for the guy.

"That's . . . *cool*," I said, trying not to sound too judgy. "I mean, I'm not going to tell or anything." I picked up the rock-hard empanada by the chimney. "Hey, if you're hungry . . . It's chicken. Fresh off the roof."

"Gracias, but the first one you threw in here left a king-size chipote on my forehead. I prefer goat, anyway."

"I've got other snacks over there." I pointed at my trusty cooler, which was sitting next to the chimney, loaded with a glorious array of my favorite junk food. "Edible stuff, too. *Unlike* my abuela's cooking . . ."

From deep in the branches, I thought I heard the kid laugh—or at least sort of hiss. But since he didn't ask me what kinda goodies I was packing, I figured he probably wasn't too hungry.

Señor Rooster started squawking again. Far away, something howled. And then, so fast it was almost silly, the temperature began to drop. I mean, it just *plummeted*. Thunder rumbled across the sky, and the wind, picking up now, swept in the first cold droplets of rain.

Guess he really does have a nose for bad weather. "Hey, man, I should probably get inside," I said. "My grandma'll be back any segundo now, and I've got a feeling she's going to throw the kitchen sink at me. *Literally.* You should probably get out of that tree, too. Looks like it's going to lightning."

And right as I said that—*zap!*—it did. A sizzling arc flashed in the clouds above the tree, turning the world first gray, then white, then a bright, brilliant blue—

And my breath stopped.

My heart stopped.

My *ENTIRE WORLD* stopped!

Because there, against the trunk of the huge pine, like a burglar or a ginormous squirrel, all long and skinny and scraggly looking, was the *strangest* creature I'd ever seen . . .

It clung silently to the tree trunk, staring back at me with a neck that twisted all the way around like an owl's.

One of its ears was short.

The other long.

One of its eyes was blue.

The other green.

It had two arms.

Two legs.

Two feet.

And it was wearing sneakers.

Converse. High-tops.

Just like me.

But that was pretty much all I saw before the lightning bolt vanished, and the world went dark again, and my heart began beating again—faster and faster. At the same time, my still-stunned mind started about the ridiculous business of trying to convince my eyes that they hadn't really just seen what they thought they'd seen.

Only I knew they had.

And what they'd seen was *a monster*!

CHAPTER 3

Someone screamed, "BAAAAAHHHHH!"

It might've been me.

Okay, it was *definitely* me.

One second, I was on the roof. The next, I was blowing through the front door of my grandparents' house like a hurricane!

It was my best Speedy Gonzales impersonation. And in my head, I was all like, "¡Ándale, ándale! ¡Arriba, arriba!"

Inside, I found both my grandparents chillaxing in the living room. My grandma was sitting on her favorite sillón, rocking and reading a magazine, and my grandpa was zonked out on the couch.

I decided to alert my abuela first, since she was the more warlike of the two. Plus, she was the only one currently conscious.

I ran right up to her, screaming, "GRANDMA, GRANDMA—THERE'S SOMETHING OUT THERE! A MONSTER! IN THE PINE TREE! IT TALKED TO ME!"

But did she even bother looking up? Nope.

"Get out of my light," she said dryly.

Get out of her—? "GRANDMA, DID YOU HEAR WHAT I JUST *SAID*?"

"Yeah, bobo, I heard it. Now I'm trying to *forget* it." Large brown eyes, so much like my mother's, glared at me from over the top of the magazine. "And you're still in my light."

For a moment, all I could do was blink at her. Seriously. Was I on some kind of hidden-camera prank show right now . . . ? "Grandma, are you *seriously* just going to sit there? I'm telling you that there's a *monster* in the *pine tree*!"

"No, there's not," she said. "There's only *one* monster around here, and I'm staring at it!" (For the record, she was staring at *me*.) "And next time you climb on my roof," she continued, "you won't be seeing no monsters, you'll be seeing *stars*. Because I'm coming up with my *frying pan*!"

Uh-huh. Definitely time for plan B.

So I whirled. I crouched. I shouted, "Grandpa, ¡despiértate! *Wake up!*"

"Ha! Keep dreaming," said my abuela, laughing. "Because I know *he* sure will."

I ignored her. "Patricio, wake up, dude! There's un monstruo in the pine tree!"

And his reaction to this terrifying news?

Behind me, Grandma grunted out a laugh. "Big-city gallito probably saw an *itty-bitty* little squirrel and thought it was some huge, scary *monstruo* . . . *pfft*! Where's she been raising this kid? In a playpen?"

Patricio snorted, then buried his sleepy face in the cushions again and went back to counting piñatas.

Yep, it was official. My grandparents put the *o* in loco. Both *o*'s! I mean, why didn't they *believe* me? Though, in their defense, *I* almost didn't believe me.

"Too bad the monster doesn't eat misbehaving little brats," my abuela grumbled as I scrambled past her to the window. "Sure would've saved me plenty of trouble."

Pretending I didn't hear, I flipped the light switch.

Outside, both post lanterns snapped on. Harsh white light flooded the yard and ran all the way up to the pointy peak of the pine.

With my face pressed up against the glass, I could see the entire tree pretty much to the trunk. But what I didn't see was anything *in* that tree. No "itty-bitty" squirrels. No scrawny kid. And *especially* no monster.

My eyes frantically scanned the yard and the field beyond it, and the acres and acres of dusty nothing-ness beyond that.

Nada. There was just nothing out there!

Not up in the tree, and not for miles and miles.

Then several realizations hit me all at once:

CHAPTER 4

The nightmare continued the following morning. I woke up in Boca Falls, New Mexico. In my grandparents' house. In a shabby little space that was more closet than room and more mousehole than closet, with my abuelo chainsawing a tree stump just outside the window, and my abuela banging on the door, telling me to get up and get ready for school.

After desayuno (self-serve milk and no-name corn-flakes), I tried calling my mom to tell her about my little breakdown the night before. But all I got was her voicemail. No big surprise, either. I knew she was going to ghost me. Because I knew that *she* knew I'd be calling her any minute now, begging to come home. In other words, she was expecting me to lay a major guilt trip on her, and she wasn't about to give me the chance. My mom was smart like that.

Anyway, my grandma had signed me up at some snooty-falooty private school on the other side of town, past the big railroad tracks. It was one of those places that was so stuck-up and bigheaded that they actually referred to themselves as a "Preparatory Academy for Excellence and Learning" instead of what they actually were, which was just a plain old middle school.

The place looked like a cross between a museum and some fancy downtown mall. And most of the kids looked like they'd stepped out of airbrushed magazine ads for the stupid stores *inside* that stupid mall.

I'm not going to lie, though. I *was* kinda nervous. That always happened to me on the first day at a new school. And considering I'd had lots of first days at new schools, it had happened to me *a lot*. But today was the worst. Because here at Pemberly, I wasn't just new, I was *different*, too. The way I looked. Even the way I talked.

I might as well have had a giant flashing neon sign over my head calling me out as the new kid.

Heck, I'd barely stepped a sneaker onto school

property, and already I could feel everybody's eyes on me and hear their sneaky lips whispering about me behind my back.

Awesome. Thanks, Mom!

In the main office, I got a printed schedule of all my classes from a prickly faced counselor wearing an ugly turtleneck, and a couple of dirty looks from two kids wearing the unofficial school uniform: pressed khakis and polo shirts. I was rocking my Lakers T-shirt and beat-up jean shorts. I fit right in.

Anyway, just as I'd expected, homeroom was a yawn. First-period math was a snooze. Second-period social studies was a total bore fest. Don't even get me started on third period. And my fourth-period science teacher, Mrs. Dwilner, couldn't have talked a vampire out of a field of garlic.

When the fifth-period bell rang, I decided to be fashionably tardy, seeing as I was beginning to notice a pattern in this place, and seeing as I really had to *pee*.

The halls were pretty much empty and my bladder was pretty much full by the time I'd navigated my way through the maze of hanging posters and gleaming green lockers and finally found a bathroom.

There was just one little problem. Or rather, ten *big* ones.

A gang of kids was gathered in front of the door labeled boys, blocking my way. Soccer players, it looked like. And probably eighth graders, too. They were all big and hairy and perfectly coordinated in their matching gray shirts and matching gray-striped shorts.

And at first, I thought they were talking about an upcoming game or something. But the longer I listened, the more it sounded like they were talking about school stuff—y'know, homework or a quiz or something.

So I said, "Hey, could you guys move study hall over a couple feet? I got an appointment with a urinal that can't really wait."

When they all ignored me, I said louder, "Yo, could you all *move*? Nature's calling and pretty soon it's going to be *flowing*."

"Go find another bathroom, nerd," problema número tres said without even bothering to turn. "We're busy."

"But I've got to pee!" I shouted.

My fingers squeezed the straps of my book bag.

I bounced anxiously on my toes.

Nobody cared.

But that's when I finally realized what was *really* going on here ...

Because that's when I spotted the one-of-these-is-not-like-the-others kid.

He definitely didn't look like a soccer player, and he definitely didn't look like an eighth grader. What he looked like was about my age, and scared, with jet-black hair that stuck straight up, rooster-comb style, and tanned skin. His clothes were kind of dorky (white knee socks, plaid shorts, what looked like a big Star Trek pin on grandad's matching plaid suspenders), and he was giving off some *serious* helpless-little-lamb vibes.

Okay, maybe he didn't look *that* much like a lamb . . . but he certainly looked worried.

And, as it turned out, he had good reason to be. Because just then, one of the jerks—er, *jocks*—snatched a folder out of his hand and shoved him back against the door. *Hard.*

"How many times I gotta explain this to you, dweeb? You gotta try and make *your* handwriting look like *my* handwriting! It ain't rocket science!" Meaty jock fingers crushed the collar of the kid's shirt while meaty jock arms lifted him right off his feet. "Or maybe you need another dip in the ole porcelain throne to help flush the wax out of your ears!"

No big surprise, the gang of soccer goons all burst into hoots and howls over that. *Punks.*

"But I did try, Zane!" said the scared little lambkin, feet dangling. "I've *been* trying!"

Scowling, the big bully smacked him on the head. "Well, obviously not hard enough, Ernie! You're gonna get me busted. *Again!* Is that what you want? Me, *suspended*?"

The kid—Ernie, I guess—sort of hesitated like he wasn't sure whether that was a trick question.

Then, watching the overgrown burro's scowl

crank up a couple of notches, he quickly said, "No, Zane! No way! You know how much I appreciate the humiliation and childhood trauma caused by our little get-togethers. My therapist says the effects should only last into my early forties."

"So then what's the problem, dork?" snarled the bully. And he slammed the kid against the wall again—*bang!*—and he smacked him upside the head again—*whap!*—and finally I just couldn't take it anymore.

Not only was my blood boiling from watching those Neanderthals pick on that poor chamaco, but my bladder was getting ready to *explode.*

So I pushed my way into their group, shouting, "Man, pick on someone your own size!"

And the result?

Yeah, it wasn't pretty . . .

"Who's the goof?" asked one of the jocks.

"Never seen him before," answered another.

"Probably a new kid," guessed a third.

But—*of course*—it was the biggest, meanest, hairiest one of the bunch who spoke directly to me.

The one called Zane sneered, "You lookin' to get in the game, spudz?"

Not very witty. I had a big head and dark skin, so he was basically calling me Mr. Potato Head. But then again, most bullies aren't very bright.

"Whoa, whoa, whoa—*spudz*?" I said. "I didn't know we were at that stage in our relationship where it's okay to give each other cute little nicknames. But in that case, I'll call you *ugly*."

See, that's the weird thing about me. Even though I was pretty shy in class and pretty shy with adults and pretty shy around girls—*especially* around girls— I always had a snappy comeback in my back pocket. Jokes were sort of like my verbal nunchucks. And some days, I could swing 'em like Bruce Lee.

Anyway, the big bad bully—aka Zane—dropped the kid—aka Ernie—then gave me the kind of look usually reserved for someone whose dog has just left a big steaming present on your front lawn. (And by "present," I mean a giant, stinking turd bomb.)

He said, "You wanna go, *ese*?"

Ese. Wow. Kid thinks he's a comedian.

I sighed. "Dude, seriously, you might want to toilet-bowl-flush the wax out of your *own* ears. I said to pick on someone your own size. You're, like, *two feet* taller than me! But like Forrest Gump said, 'Stupid is as stupid does,' am I right?"

You could tell from the glassy-eyed way Zane was now staring at me that he'd never seen any of the funny memes from that classic Tom Hanks movie.

It didn't really matter, though.

If you know anything about overgrown, over-muscled, and under-*brained* middle school bullies, you know at that point it was on like Donkey Kong.

I'd love to say that I went all Peter Parker and gave this bozo a "hands-on" lesson in Newton's second law (you know, mass times acceleration equals force). But it just wasn't what happened.

Sure, I *did* shove him (right after he shoved me). Only it was *his* shove—the second one—that more closely resembled the devastating two-handed power thrust of a teenage superhero with superhuman strength.

When I'd finally shaken the fuzz out of my head and blinked the stars out of my eyes, I looked around and realized that everyone had bolted—both the bullies and the bullied.

It was just me now.

Well, me and some stunned-looking, curly-haired teacher lady poking her head out of one of the classrooms.

"*WHAT DID YOU DO?*" she shrieked. Her eyes were the size of frisbees behind the thick rims of her glasses.

"*Me?*" I shouted. "Nothing! He pushed me!"

Her gaze flew up and down the empty hall. "Who? The invisible man?"

I sighed, feeling so annoyed you wouldn't believe it. I mean, why even waste time trying to convince her that it hadn't been my fault? No one ever believed me, anyway.

"Nah," I said. "It was Casper the Friendly Ghost."

CHAPTER 5

Surprise, surprise, that little sarcastic remark (and the fact that I'd completely *demolished* that shiny-looking display case full of shiny-looking trophies) had earned me a one-way ticket to the principal's office.

Ms. Jackie, the teacher who'd busted me, handed me off to a hall monitor, who handed me off to a guidance counselor, who handed me off to an office aide, who led me down two flights of stairs and into the main office, where she handed me off to another lady, who frowned disapprovingly, and tsked her tongue at me, and then sat me down inside one of those little waiting rooms outside a door with a large bronze plaque that read principal skennyrd.

The whole way over, my back had been killing me. So the whole way over I'd been all like—

But my Latina mama magic didn't seem to be working. Maybe you had to be a Latina mama to make it work?

Anyway, it was just me, a receptionist, and a girl. A sixth grader, probably. She had dark skin, wore these cool oversized glasses, and was— how do I put this?—sort of march- ing purposefully back and forth across the carpeted floor, holding up a big hand-painted sign.

I watched her stomp back and forth and back and forth, the points of her sign stabbing up toward the ceiling tiles, until finally I just couldn't help myself.

"Uh, what are you doing?" I asked.

The girl didn't stop marching. "It's kind of obvious, isn't it?"

"Is it?"

She sighed. "We're taking a stand against Principal Skennyrd's wanton glorification of the senseless and systematic slaughter of innocent animals." Seeing my confused look, she added, "We're protesting, okay?"

"Oh." I glanced around to make sure I wasn't missing any other "protesters." I wasn't. "So I keep hearing 'we,'" I said, "but I'm only seeing . . . *you*."

Her hazel eyes gave one of those super-annoyed eye rolls that girls give when they want to say, *Who in the frijoles is this dweeb?* but don't actually want to waste the breath to say it.

"There are *plenty* who are with me in spirit," she said flatly. "Besides, all great movements start with a single person." Then, digging a clipboard and pen out of her backpack, she held them out to me. "You want to be part of the problem or the solution?"

"Wh-what do you mean?"

"I mean, are you going to sign my petition or not?"

"Oh, yeah. Sure. I'm an animal lover, too."

She smiled. It was almost friendly. "That's nice."

Suddenly, the door with the big bronze plaque swung open, and the owner of that plaque loomed into view—and I'm talking *skyscraper-LOOMED*—casting a ginormous, thundercloud-like shadow over me and, well, pretty much everything else in the room.

Something told me I wasn't going to like what came next.

CHAPTER 6

"Mr. Lopez," Principal Skennyrd said (more like *growled*). "In my office. *Now!*"

Okay. I've got to be honest. Never in my entire life had I seen a principal this dude's size. In fact, I'd never seen *anyone* this dude's size! Not on TV. Not in the WWE. *Nowhere.* He wasn't just *ginormously* tall—the man was legit buff! Heck, he made the Rock look like the Pebble! Honestly, the "person" he most closely resembled was probably Bruce Banner. And that was only *after* he turned green.

At any rate, since I usually made it a point not to argue with people who looked like they could bench-press an Escalade, I got up and shouldered my backpack and dragged my feet into his office. But the second I stepped inside, I froze.

My stomach dropped down to my toes.

My heart jumped up into my throat.

I tried to swallow. Or breathe. Or turn around and run. But I couldn't do any of that! Why not, you ask? Because I'd never seen any room like it in my entire life!

It was . . . it was . . .

It was like going on a safari . . . in a *horror* movie!

The office of DEATH

Apparently, there wasn't a single species of animal on the face of the planet that this guy didn't think should be turned into an office decoration.

I was suddenly very happy I'd signed that girl's petition.

"Sit down, Mr. Lopez," Skennyrd ordered.

He eyed me as I sat down on one of those butt-breaking plastic desk chairs, and I eyed him back as he settled himself behind a desk so wide and so wrapped in fuzzy black-and-white cowhide that it honestly looked like something he'd hunted down and killed in the wild.

The desk was covered with all the typical junk you find on a principal's desk—the typical papers and pencils, the typical staplers and scissors and sticky notes.

But there was also something you typically *never* find: a Rambo-style hunting arrow. Short but deadly looking, resting on a little wooden sword shelf, the kind people use to display samurai swords.

Skennyrd caught me staring at it and said, "Looking's fine, but don't you even think about touching. That's my lucky arrow. I brought down my first Sumatran two-horned rhinoceros with it. The serrated arrowhead's coated with approximately four hundred milligrams of rattlesnake venom. Enough to cause full-body paralysis in a grown adult in less than thirty seconds."

"Okay, that's not creepy at all," I said. "But, uh, listen. About the whole display-case thing, it wasn't even my—"

"In *this* office," Skennyrd boomed, shouting right over me, "you will speak *only* when spoken to! Do I make myself absolutely clear?" He didn't wait for me to answer. "You speak out of turn again and I'll suspend you. You lie to me and I'll suspend you. You give me any snarky looks or even the slightest hint of sass and I'll suspend you so fast it'll make your eyeballs spin Hula-Hoops around that big head of yours. As a matter of fact, I'm not seeing an awful lot of ways you walk back out that door still a member of this prestigious student body."

Prestigious. *Pfft.* Like I gave a rat's behind.

"What happened with the display case on the second floor?" Skennyrd asked sharply.

"¡Me empujaron! Some overgrown mocoso named Zane pushed me into it!"

"Ms. Jackson says she didn't see anyone but you in the hall."

"Well, you didn't ask me what Ms. Jackson saw, you asked me what *actually* happened."

Skennyrd's cinder-block-shaped jaw tightened. In

a voice usually reserved for *Off with his head!* or *To the gallows with 'em!*, he said, "You have a smart mouth, Mr. Lopez."

Órale . . . Here we go again. "I've always thought that's better than having a dumb one, no?"

The beady eyes peering steadily out of his massive, pale face didn't leave mine. "You'd be surprised." Then, running a giant hand over the blondish-gray fuzz of his buzz cut, he leaned back in his chair and said, "Mr. Lopez, what we have here at Pemberly is a tier-one learning institute with a long legacy of tradition and academic excellence. This is *the* top-ranked private school in the entire southwestern United States. Under my leadership, we have won countless awards, numerous honors, and have remained an institution free from distraction and all forms of juvenile delinquency. And I intend to keep it that way, Mr. Lopez.

"Allow me to give you the lay of the land, so to speak. Make things plain for you. Your obvious contempt for authority annoys me. Your blatant violation of the school dress code annoys me. You speaking Spanish in my office annoys me. But most of all, Mr. Lopez, *you* annoy me. The only reason you were even allowed through our illustrious doors is because of an old and quite frankly *ridiculous* school policy, which states that we must, for a probationary period, accept the children of townsfolk who live within a fifteen-mile radius of the school. Unfortunately, your grandparents' farm happens to fall just within that limit. Had it not, you, Mr. Lopez, wouldn't have ever *breathed* Pemberly air; that much I can assure you."

His gaze dropped to an open manila folder on his desk. "I see here that you recently served a Saturday detention. You were also recently disciplined for shoving a fellow student, correct?"

"Yeah, but that was only because that bobo thought it'd be hilarious to pour half a bottle of Elmer's glue into my backpack!" I said. (Long story.) "What was I supposed to do?"

Skennyrd, meanwhile, just sat there like a scowling mountain, eyeing me the same sort of way an angry orc might eye a helpless hobbit. "That's your problem, Mr. Lopez. It's never your fault, is it? Someone else always starts it. Well, let me make something abundantly clear to you: I don't care who starts it, because in this school, I'm *always* the one who finishes it."

Thump! He closed the folder and then leaned

forward, steepling fingers the size of rolling pins.

"You see, Jorge, I'm an educator by profession, a disciplinarian by disposition, but a hunter at heart. I've traveled to all the huntable continents and taken down all the big game this planet has to offer. In fact, I'm one of only two hunters in the last ten years to win both the prestigious Weatherby Award and the Ovis World Slam. Quite an accomplishment, if I do say so myself. Now, you're probably asking yourself, 'Why is he telling me this?'"

I wasn't, actually. But that didn't stop him.

"And the reason is because, not surprisingly, children and wild animals share many of the very same fight-or-flight instincts. Which is to say that the very same qualities which make a great hunter *also* make a great principal. A hunter must possess patience. A principal must possess patience. A hunter must know their prey. A principal must know their students. Above all, a hunter must be willing to lie in ambush for their prey, in much the same way that a principal must be willing to lie in wait for the more subversive elements of their student body."

The corners of his mouth curled into a mean-looking grin, and he squinted his left eye as if taking aim at me down the barrel of some invisible rifle.

"So color me waiting, Mr. Lopez. And understand this: if you step so much as another *toe* out of line, I promise you that the next head going up on my wall is going to be *yours*."

CHAPTER 7

"So how'd you like your new school?" asked Grandpa as I walked—all right, *stomped*—up the long gravel driveway to the house.

I stopped beside his beat-up pickup, where he was unloading some cement sacks and rolls of chicken wire.

"I didn't," I said. "It stinks."

And I wasn't even being all dramatic, either. Besides the whole trophy-case debacle, everyone had basically given me the "new kid" treatment, keeping a good ten feet away like I had lice or something, and pretty much no one talked to me.

Oh, except for Liza, the one-girl revolution I'd met in the office, and Ernie, the kid I'd sort of saved from the soccer bullies. They were both in my last two periods. I think they'd both said hi.

Tossing another cement sack on the ground, Grandpa paused for a moment to wipe the sweat off his face. "Bueno, I've got a pine tree air freshener in the truck you can hang off the corner of your desk if it's that bad."

Groaning, I rolled my eyes. "No, Abuelo. I don't mean stinks, like it *smells*. I mean stinks, as in the kids are awful and the teachers are awful and the principal is even more awful than all of 'em put *together*." Still mad frustrated, I kicked a rock at the back tire of the truck. It clanged off the dented hubcap. "And not to mention the fact that it was only my *first day* and they gave me a pile of homework so tall it could choke a jirafa!"

My grandpa looked impressed. "Is that right?"

"Uh-huh. But I'm not going to do any of it," I said, crossing my arms in my best *try me* pose. "They can all go fly a papalote if they think I'm wasting my time with that mess."

My grandpa looked even more impressed. "Is that right?"

"Yeah, that's right. After three o'clock, I'm a free man. Homework is for the birds, anyway."

Patricio was nodding his head now, like he totally got where I was coming from. "A free man, huh? And so what are you going to do with all your free time, Mr. *Free Man*?"

I shrugged. "Probably hook up my Nintendo to that crummy old TV in my room. Play some Mario Kart."

"Oye, why don't you help me out a little first? It's hot out here."

"Oh, c'mon, Abuelo. Do I have to?"

"No, you don't *haaaaave* to," he said, poking fun at me. "But your grandma isn't going to let you just sit around the house playing video games. It's either this or she'll stick you in the kitchen de-feathering chickens." He nodded toward the chicken coop behind the house. "She just sent Santiago and Camilla to chicken heaven, God rest their poor little chicken souls."

I gaped. "Grandpa, are you being serious right now?"

His meaty shoulders shrugged. "Don't believe me, go 'head. Go inside. Take your chances. Maybe you'll enjoy plucking plumas."

On second thought, it looked like Mario and Luigi were going to have to drive their own carts for a while.

"Quick. Hand me one of those shovels," I said. "Before Grandma strangles any more chickens!"

CHAPTER 8

TWENTY-FIVE MINUTES LATER

Man, how do you do it?

It's easy when you don't have a choice.

I looked up at him, squinting against the blazing New Mexican sun. "What do you mean, 'you don't have a choice'? It's still a free country, isn't it?"

"Sure it is. But not all of us are free to choose."

"What's that supposed to mean?"

"Means I wasn't lucky like you. I never got a chance to go to school, to learn how to read or write. I've been working construction since I was diez añitos, so I could help my mother feed all your little tíos y tías. I wasn't blessed like you to have a school so close by, full of teachers that wanted to teach me things." He took a swig of water. His dark eyes looked deeply into mine. "Yeah, it's a free country, and yeah, some of us are free to choose, but even then, you only get two choices: you either work with your head or you work with your hands."

Now he held his hands out to me, turning them over slowly.

His palms were rough with calluses, crisscrossed with deep wrinkles and scars. They ran across his skin like the course of some wild river. And in them, I thought I could see the whole course of his life, all his years and all his hard work.

Man, it hurt just *looking* at them . . .

"But like I said," whispered my abuelo, "you're

blessed. You at least get to choose: hands or head. So make sure you make a choice you'll be happy with when you're my age."

For what felt like a long time, I just sat there, staring up at my grandpa in the scorching heat with sweat beading on my forehead and hot sweat running into my eyes.

I wondered which of the two he would choose if he could do it all over again.

I wondered what fifty-year-old me would say to current me.

I just sat there, wondering.

"Bueno, you're done here," Patricio said with a sigh. "I'll finish up." He turned back to look at me. "So what are you going to do now? Play your video games?"

My first thought was, *You betcha!* I mean, it's what I'd been looking forward to all day. But then I looked down at my dusty, dirty, aching hands and felt the grit under my fingernails and the soreness in my lower back, and suddenly my thinking changed.

"I, uh, actually I'll probably check out some of my homework and stuff first," I told him. "You know, see what all the fuss is about."

I watched the corners of my grandpa's eyes crinkle in a sun-toasted smile. His eyes, the same shade of brown as mine, were as happy as I'd ever seen them.

"Qué inteligente," he said.

CHAPTER 9

The homework was even tougher than I'd expected. And I had some pretty high expectations. There were a million "critical reading questions" at the end of every chapter, and the math stuff might as well have been explained using Egyptian hieroglyphics. I was pretty sure I'd sprained a finger (and probably a few brain cells) just trying to work through some of the sample problems.

On a positive note, I did recognize a few of the symbols. The teacher had been going over them in class. Problem was, when she'd asked if anyone didn't get how they worked, I'd been too embarrassed to raise my hand. I hadn't wanted all the other kids to know that I didn't know, and so nothing had changed. I *still* didn't know.

Funny how that works, huh?

At any rate, I told myself that all I needed was a quick little pick-me-up. Something scrumptious and sweet, like a Rice Krispies Treat, to shut my grumbling stomach up and zap my snoozing brain. But when I went looking for my cooler, it was a total no-show.

And it didn't take me long to figure out why, either: I'd left it up on the roof last night!

If it hadn't been my own face, I would've slapped myself. *Seriously.* That's how stupid I felt!

And with this New Mexico heat, I guess I'll be drinking that Rice Krispies Treat...

Outside, the sun was already beginning to melt like a bright orange egg yolk into the frying pan of the horizon when I snuck out the back door to get my cooler.

Silently, like a Chicano ninja, I climbed the little lemon tree again and pulled myself up onto the roof. But the moment I was up there, I couldn't help sweeping my eyes anxiously around for the *you-know-what.*

The good news: I didn't see any more imaginary monsters.

The bad news: I didn't see my cooler, either. It

wasn't by Señor Rooster,
it wasn't by the gutter, it wasn't
anywhere!

Climbing down, I decided
to do some investigaing. And
guess what I found? The crum-
pled remains of a candy-bar
wrapper—my king-size Butterfinger—
inside my abuela's window planter!

And that wasn't all I found, either . . .

It reminded me of that old children's story
"Hansel and Gretel," when those two silly
kids (you guessed it, Hansel and Gretel)
leave a trail of bread crumbs in the woods.

Only instead of bread crumbs, someone
had left a trail of junk food crumbs and wrappers. *My* junk food. Which meant they had jacked
my cooler!

It *had* to be the monster.
Oh, c'mon, dude! Please
don't start with that again!
I scolded myself. *There is*

no monstruo. There never WAS un monstruo!

Well, there might not be a monster around here, but there sure as heck was a thief.

Now, I know what you're thinking. *Jorge, it's just a cooler. Who cares?*

And had that cooler not been my favorite cooler, and had it not had the logo of my favorite baseball team stickered on the side (go, Dodgers!), or been loaded with all my favorite go-to snacks, I probably wouldn't have cared. Except it *was* my favorite cooler and it *did* have the logo of my favorite baseball team, and I'd spent a whole week and almost a whole *thirty dollars* loading it with the crème de la crème of junky, sugary treats!

Which meant I did care. I cared a lot, in fact.

In my mind, all I could see was some grubby-fingered punk chowing down on my hard-earned, hand-picked goodies, and I felt myself grow caliente with anger.

Whoever they were—wherever they'd gone—they weren't getting away with this.

CHAPTER 10

Needless to say, the thief had been sloppy. Very sloppy. They might as well have left a giant cartoony sign on the lawn that read i went thataway!

Every couple of yards, I'd find either a candy-bar wrapper or a piece of bubble gum, a crumble of potato chips or a sprinkle of cookie.

I followed the trail of junk food like a bloodhound tracking a hot scent; and eventually it led me into a stretch of thick woods, maybe a quarter of a mile from the southwest edge of my grandparents' property.

About ten yards in, I discovered the shriveled, silvery carcass of a Capri Sun. It looked like the final "bread crumb" of the trail. I didn't see any more wrappers or bottles or crumbs anywhere.

The little plastic straw was still glued to the back,

but the pouch itself had been sucked dry. *Completely* dry. And just as I flipped it over with the tips of my fingers, trying to avoid the swarm of creepy-crawlies hunting for a sugar fix, I froze.

On the flip side of the pouch, below the surfer kid and above the big orange sun, were a pair of gashes.

No, not gashes . . . more like *puncture holes.*

Two of them. And big ones. Big and circular—perfectly circular—and unmistakably *FANG-LIKE!*

Question: Ever seen something so mind-meltingly scary that the entire world around you just *stops*?

Well, it was like that. And suddenly, the woods seemed to go very still and very, *very* quiet.

It was a terrifying sight.

It really was.

But not *nearly* as terrifying as what I saw next . . .

CHAPTER 11

Twilight was coming in fast, but even in the near dark, I could see it clearly. Crouching just on the other side of a stand of scrubby trees, crunching away on my brand-new tube of BBQ Pringles, was a big, dirty, hairy, forest-dwelling creature.

Except . . . this wasn't your *typical* big, dirty, hairy, forest-dwelling creature.

No, my amigos, *this* was a monster. The exact monster I'd seen up in my grandparents' tree!

So it wasn't a hallucination, after all . . .

With that realization came another—an even more terrifying one: this kind of monster had a name! A name known all over the world, as a matter of fact!

It started with a "chupa" and ended with a "cabra." *A chupacabra!* That's what that thing was!

I'd watched enough TV shows on undiscovered cryptids and scary local *leyendas* to be *absolutely* positive about it, too.

These *monstruos* were basically the bloodsucking equivalent of Sasquatch! They were vicious! And bloodthirsty! And responsible for thousands, if not *millions*, of brutal vampire attacks all over the Americas and even as far as Puerto Rico!

There were even rumors that those things could suck every last ounce of blood out of a human body before you could even feel the sting of their fangs!

Chupacabra . . .

The name—not to mention all the horrifying imagery that came with it—echoed through my mind like a coyote cry in the Mojave.

Now, you're probably thinking, *Jorge, whatever you do, do NOT run, dude!*

Which is solid advice. Nine out of ten zoologists would probably tell you that running from a wild, dangerous animal (or, in this case, a wild, dangerous *monster*) isn't really such a hot idea.

Unfortunately, it happened to be my only idea . . .

I was hauling nachas before I even realized it. Branches slapped at my face and sliced at my arms as I flew wildly through the woods, zigging and zagging and stumbling between the trees. Pine needles went *crunch!* under my sneakers. I heard something crash through a tangle of bushes to my left, and I ran like I was running for my life. Which, in this case, I literally was!

As I came bursting out of the trees, I stopped running. I whirled. My eyes scanned left, right, left. The woods were dark. Totally dark and totally featureless.

I didn't see anything. No creatures lurking in the gloom. No glowing red eyes peering out at me from the deep shadows. Where had that thing gone? Was it still chasing me?

Had it even *been* chasing me?

I could've sworn it was, but—

Lights—harsh and yellow—washed over me like a flood.

I realized I was standing in the middle of a road.

Then I heard the wild blare of a car horn, but it was too late. What looked like a monster truck was barreling straight for me, huge and gray and completely unavoidable!

Frozen like a deer in headlights!

All I had time to do was squeeze my eyes shut. So that's all I did.

But at the exact moment I did—*wham!*—something slammed into me.

I flew a few feet to the side, falling onto my hands and knees on the roadside. The screech of tires split the air.

Then there was a loud *clunk!* And a split second later, something went tumbling past me, into the high grass.

I watched as a huge shadowy figure pushed itself

Yeah, that actually happens in real life . . .

slowly up, and then—even more slowly—slunk off into the night.

And *that's* when all the puzzle pieces came together for me.

The truck hadn't hit me.

I was still alive. Alive and *unsquashed*!

And the monster?

Well, it had saved my life.

CHAPTER 12

"*What in the smelted snake sausages was that thing?*" roared the driver, scrambling out of the truck and waving some stupid little toy rifle around.

The skinny metal barrel winked in the moonlight as I pushed unsteadily to my feet. "What thing?"

"The thing *chasin'* you, boy!"

Hold up. I recognized that voice.

Then I recognized the massive pale face the voice was coming from!

"Skennyrd," I breathed.

"You," he growled, narrowing those rattlesnake eyes on me. In his enormous mitts, the rifle still looked toy-size; but this close, anyone who had ever seen a toy rifle before could've easily told ya it was no toy.

"Uh, *hi!*"

Skennyrd's lips pulled back from his teeth in a

vicious snarl. "Running out into the middle of a street at night? How *estúpido* can you be?"

I didn't say anything.

"And what the heck was after you?" he shouted, scanning the dark roadside and the darker trees beyond.

"There wasn't, uh, anything after me." I'm not sure why I lied. Maybe it was the very real possibility of walking into Skennyrd's office one of these days, seeing a "familiar face" up on his wall, and knowing that I'd had something to do with it.

"BOY, DO I LOOK LIKE GEPPETTO TO YOU?" he exploded.

"Gep—who?"

"GEPPETTO! DOES MY VISAGE OVERLY RESEMBLE THE IMPOVERISHED, ELDERLY WOODCARVER'S, OR NOT?"

Is he talking about the dude from the fairy tale? "Um, no?"

"THEN WHY ARE YOU TRYING TO PINOC-CHIO ME LIKE I'M GEPPETTO?" He was in a rage now, the veins of his tree-trunk-thick neck and arms standing out like cords. The guy honestly looked like a bull getting ready to charge. "OF COURSE SOMETHING WAS CHASING YOU! I *HIT* IT!"

"I—I don't think you did," I said.

"It makes no difference *what* you think, son! Look at my fender!"

Squinting against the glare of the headlights, I looked. And yep, there was a big, ugly dimple in the polished aluminum . . . I could see my own scared reflection staring back at me, all stretchy and out of whack, like one of those not-so-fun fun house mirrors. Mosquitos buzzed around my ears.

Skennyrd said, "See, there's a dent in it and there *ain't* one in you, which just about settles that, don't you think?" His predatory eyes drifted past me, scanning the dark roadside again. "Besides, I *saw* the thing . . ."

"M-maybe it was a stray dog," I tried.

His burning gaze shifted slowly back to me. His manhole-cover-size nostrils flared. He wasn't blinking.

"Maybe it was sleeping by the roadside and got scared when you hit the brakes," I said, wiping nervous sweat out of my eyes.

The hunter's mouth had hardened into a skeptical frown. He still hadn't blinked. At last he said, "A stray dog, huh?"

Clearly, he wasn't buying it.

Unfortunately for him, I didn't really give a flip.

CHAPTER 13

That was the last thing Skennyrd said to me. He
didn't even ask if I was lost or hurt or needed a ride
home. Nada. He just scowled at me and scowled at
the damage to his fender and scowled at the trees and
the road and the tall swaying grass, and even scowled
down at his rifle, before climbing back into his truck
and speeding off.

Once he was gone (and I could no longer see the
red pinpricks of his taillights), I walked carefully,
cautiously out into the tall grass. Out to where I'd last
seen the creature.

You know how they say curiosity killed the cat?
Well, mine was probably about to get me turned into
monster chow. Still, I couldn't help it. I had to see that
thing again.

All around me, the wind whistled and the wild

grass rolled like a sleepy sea, reminding me of the waves back in Santa Monica. The bright full moon shone down, painting everything a ghostly blue.

I'd made it maybe fifteen yards when a low moan rose above the soft rustle of the grass.

And suddenly, I spotted it!

Only at first, all I really saw was a pair of glowing eyes. One green, the other blue. They blinked and stared, watching me warily through the gloom.

Then the wind blew harder, parting the grass around me, and I saw the rest of the thing: the long, scraggly body and the longer, scragglier, twiglike legs that ended at a pair of beat-up sneakers.

It wasn't moving. Blood matted the fur of its left arm. One of its legs had been . . . I don't know what. It looked like it had gotten bent out of shape doing some guru-level yoga move. The monster looked sad and scared and pretty badly injured.

But the sight of those Count Dracula fangs—Dios mío, those things were huge!—still sent a pulse of fear skidding through me.

I was about half a second away from showing the creature my nachas again when another low, whimpering moan crawled out from deep inside the thing. It sounded like some little kid trying to get up after a bad bike wreck. And just like that, all my fear melted into concern.

I just felt sorry for the thing. I really did. It had, after all, ended up like that by saving *me*.

I risked another step closer. "¿Estás bien?" I whispered. "Are you okay?"

"'Okay'?" The mismatched eyes flicked first to its twisted leg, then to its bloody side, and then glared up at me. "Never better."

"Does anything feel . . . broken?"

"No."

"You want to try moving?"

"No."

"Are you going to . . . die?"

"I hope not. But you keep askin' questions and maybe I change my mind."

Huh. At least "it" seemed to have a sense of humor. After a moment I asked, "Why'd you save me?"

"Who says I saved you?"

"I did. You pushed me out of the way of the truck."

Skinny shoulders shrugged. "Thought I saw a baby goat in the road. You were just in the way."

That got a smile out of me. "Nah, I don't think so. You saved me on purpose. How come?"

It shrugged again. "Blame it on animal instincts."

"So, you're an . . . animal?"

"I'm not from outer space, if dat's what you're wonderin'."

"But you . . . talk." Call me Captain Obvious, but whatever. I guess you could say that the freakishness of hearing something that hairy (and that *fang*-toothed) speak my language—speak *any* language!—was starting to sink in.

"Yeah, and?" said the monster. "So do you."

"But what kind of animal are you, then?"

Its curly fur bristled as it scowled at me. "¡Venga! You don't quit, eh?"

"Not really."

El monstruo looked annoyed. Muy, muy annoyed. But it also looked secretly happy to have someone to talk to.

Finally, it gave in and said, "I believe *your* kind calls *my* kind chupacabras. But we call you all chupadedos, so that makes us even."

I knew it! He was a giant bloodsucker! "Your name is Carter, right? You were up in my grandma's tree last night."

It wasn't so much a question. I knew it was him. More like I just needed to say the words out loud to help my panicking brain wrap itself around the total *loco-ness* of it all.

I mean, I was literally having a conversation with a real-life *chupacabra*! How awesome/scary/amazing/ surreal/*TERRIFYING* was that?!

"Yeah, my name is Carter," whispered the chupacabra, wincing and grabbing at his side again.

"Dude, I think you need help."

"And I think you need to leave me alone," he grunted. "I'm fine."

"You don't *look* fine."

"It's jess a scratch. Lemme lie here in paz, okay? I be good come mañana."

Just then, a spear of bright light sliced through the grass maybe five yards from where we were. I squatted down as the beam swept through the swaying stalks, passing right over us.

A truck was rolling slowly by, the driver working a window-mounted spotlight.

Skennyrd!

Yep, definitely him. There was no mistaking that evil-looking truck, or the even eviler-looking refrigerator-width figure sitting behind the steering wheel.

"You aren't going to last till mañana," I told the chupacabra.

"What?"

"You can't stay here."

"Why not?"

"That's my principal!"

The monster looked at me like I was a few green peppers short of a fajita. "You mean, it's a rule of yours to never leave a wounded animal behind?"

"No, not my princi*ple*—my princi*pal*! I'm pretty sure he saw you before, and I'm pretty sure he's trying to see you again. Only by 'see' I mean *stuff* and *mount* you up on his wall! He's some kind of trophy hunter."

"¡Vaya! Did you say *hunter*?" That got the chupacabra sitting up real fast. "Como *BIG-GAME* hunter?"

"Exactly like one," I said.

"Hombre, *I'm* big game! I can't stay here!"

"That's what I'm saying!"

"So stop sayin' and start helpin'!"

"All right, all right, *chill!*"

I hunkered down, spying Skennyrd's taillights through the grass. He was making a turn at the end of the road, which probably meant he was planning on swinging back around again.

Sí, señor, it was definitely time to shake our tail feathers.

CHAPTER 14

Fun fact: The only pets I'd ever had growing up were stray dogs. I'd lure them into my backyard with pieces of hot dog, my mom and I would give them a home, and they'd give us their love. It was cool. But the last time I'd brought home a stray, it had bitten one of our neighbors, which had gotten us thrown out of our town house.

After that, my mom had dropped her mommy gavel. "No more perros callejeros!" she'd decreed. She had even made me pinky promise. Which, as everyone knows, kind of made it a forever promise. But in all fairness, I'd never made any promises about stray *monsters*.

The toolshed behind my grandparents' house looked like the sort of place that had been built before Thomas Edison invented the light bulb. It only had one window, and the walls and floors were made of rickety old planks. It smelled of dust and it smelled of rust. And now, as I helped the huge, hairy, limping cryptid through the slumping door, it smelled of chupacabra, too. (And let me just say, *PEEEE-YEW!*)

The monster sounded worried. "It's a little . . . claustrophobic, ¿sabes?"

"'Claustrophobic'? What were you expecting, four

bedrooms and a swimming pool? It's a toolshed, bro. You're lucky you don't have a possum for a room-mate."

A very thin, very hairy finger pointed at the rake in the corner. "Dat's rusted," he said. "You can get teta-nus from dat."

"Well, no one said you had to scratch your back with it, man! Here, sit down." I'd spotted one of those foldable outdoor lounge chairs and set it up for him.

Once he got that lanky, Chester Cheetah–esque body of his nice and settled, the chupacabra looked up at me and grinned. Well, at least showed more fang. "Qué padre."

"See? Okay, so listen. I'll come check up on you tomorrow after school. But I've got to get back before my abuela starts wondering where I went. Forget big-game hunters, that lady is the *real* apex predator around here. She can maim and kill with just foot-wear."

Carter looked impressed. His batlike ears twitched. His skinny catlike tail wrapped tightly around the leg of the lounge chair. "¡No manches!" Then he said, "Wait, you leavin' me alone?"

"Yeah, why?"

"It's dark."

"So?"

"And I'm un poquito . . ." His words trailed off.

"A little what?"

"A little scared of dis place, okay?"

"*You're* scared of *this* place? Bro, you're the scariest thing in here!"

His eyes—well, his green one, anyway—drifted slowly over my shoulder. "You sure 'bout that?"

I turned. Sitting on a busted shelf, crooked dust-covered legs dangling like limp spaghetti, was some kind of raggedy old rag doll. It had a button eye and tiny wooden shoes.

But in the shadows, and with the spooky way the moonlight was slanting in through cracks in the ceiling, it felt like at any moment it could turn into something like this:

"All right," I said. "So maybe you're the *second* scariest thing in here."

I saw the corners of the chupacabra's lips begin to lift in a fangy grin. But suddenly the grin twisted into a grimace as his clawed hand gripped his side. From deep inside his throat came these odd, clicking, crickety sounds. They made me think of an ancient grandfather clock on the verge of busting a pendulum and spilling its springy, metallic guts.

"Yo, you good?" I whispered.

Wincing, the scrawny goat-slurper shook his head.

"Does it hurt, like . . . a lot?"

"Yeah. Maybe it is more than a scratch, eh?"

"Uh . . . so—so what should I do? Should I call a vet or something?"

"What's dat?"

"An animal doctor."

"You know any that treat bloodsuckers?"

"No."

"Then forget it."

For a moment I just stood there, wracking my brain, trying to figure out what I could do to help this dude. This thing. This . . . *whatever*!

I said, "But don't *creatures* like you have super-human recovery ability or whatever?"

"Do I look like some cartoon superhero to you? ¡Que gracioso!"

"Wait. You watch cartoons?"

His skinny shoulders shrugged. "Sometimes. Through people's ventanas."

Huh. I'm not sure why, but the idea of him hiding out by someone's house and watching cartoons through their window made me like him even more.

I said, "But don't even regular animals recover pretty fast?"

"Uh-huh, ¿y qué? I jess got run over, like, five seconds ago!" His mouth—which, by the way, looked wide enough to stick your *whole* head inside—bent into another painful grimace as he curled up on his side. "Besides," he hissed, "to heal up from something like dis, I'm gonna need sangre."

I gulped. "Blood? You mean, like . . . a transfusion?"

"No, I mean, like, *dinner*."

Ah, right. He's a chupacabra, after all. "Well, let me see what I can do, all right? Just . . . just stay here for now. And don't make any noise. Oh, and if you happen to run into an old dude or a lady who likes to fight using her chanclas, don't suck their blood, okay? It's probably one of my grandparents. And they can be pretty selfish when it comes to their, uh, vital fluids."

Carter nodded like he got me. Whoa. Was this a first in human–chupacabra diplomacy? It seemed like it.

But as I slipped silently out of the shed, easing the door shut behind me and leaving that giant bloodsucker lounging on my grandma's busted lawn chair, you could say I started having second thoughts...

CHAPTER 15

The following day at school—ahem, I mean, the Preparatory Academy for Excellence and Learning—I was assigned a group for the upcoming school play.

The Halloween play here at Pemberly was supposedly a pretty big deal, sort of a local tradition, and the whole town showed up in the school's gigantic auditorium to watch.

All sixth graders had to participate. Most had been preparing for the last eight weeks. And Mr. Crowell, Pemberly's drama teacher, had set it up so that you got to pick if you wanted to be "front of the house"—onstage, acting—or "back of the house"—working on the props and stage design and stuff like that.

I chose back of the house, because I didn't like the idea of a bunch of strangers staring at me while

I read some silly lines, and so Mr. Crowell put me on "team wardrobe."

At first, I was kind of bummed about it. I'll admit it. I'm not one of those kids that's all into fashion or whatever. But when I found out that Ernie and Liza were also on team wardrobe, I started feeling better.

Liza and Ernie turned out to be super cool. They were loners, kind of like me, but hung out with each

other because, like most loners, they appreciated a little company. In the span of just a few minutes, they'd told me all about each other.

Yeah, they might've been a little *too* excited to have made a new friend . . .

Anyway, Ernie was Native American. He loved baseball just as much as I did—he was a huge Arizona Diamondbacks fan—and might've even loved science fiction and junk food a little more. The dude's Starship *Enterprise* backpack was so stuffed with candy bars and Jawbreakers that you would've thought he'd just pulled a heist on Willy Wonka's famous chocolate factory.

Liza, on the other hand, hated junk food and science fiction. She was a vegan. She refused to eat anything with a face—both fish and fowl were foul—and no animal byproducts whatsoever, including eggs, dairy, or honey. She claimed that her strict dietary standards kept her away from all the "dirty foods." But it sounded to me like her diet kept her away from pretty much *all* foods.

Liza was uber smart, though, and uber passionate about everything she did. Which, apparently, included wardrobe design.

Now, here's where things got even more interesting: *our* part in the play was basically to design and sew the costume for this year's villain, which—I kid you not—was a *chupacabra*!

Liza had already come up with a super-dope design, but with my wealth of "firsthand" knowledge, I was able to add a few small touches . . .

Naturally, from that point on, all I wanted to do

was spill the frijoles about Carter. It was *exactly* the sort of thing you told your friends about!

But since I didn't want them to think that I was completely off my rocker—and I was pretty sure Carter wouldn't appreciate being outed—I bit my lip and me callé la boca.

CHAPTER 16

I spent my last class, and pretty much the entire walk home, trying to figure out how I was going to get my hands on some sangre for Carter.

The most obvious answer: pay a visit to the local blood bank. But that was probably a no-go, because who ever heard of anyone going to a blood bank to *get* blood? You went there to *donate* it.

I also toyed with the idea of letting the chupacabra take a little sip from yours truly. (Desperate times call for desperate measures, right?) But the more I thought about it, the less sanitary it seemed, and the more nervous I got.

The best option was a butcher's shop. But the problem was that fresh, bloody meat wasn't cheap. So before I could score Carter a meal, I was going to have to score myself some cash.

Grandma Paz was sitting in her favorite sillón, reading *El Nuevo Herald*, when I came home from school and asked her to spot me twenty bucks.

And you would've thought I'd asked her to hand sew me an astronaut suit and fly me to Mars on a space shuttle made of *nachos*.

"*Twenty bucks?*" she shrieked, almost flinging the newspaper at me. "¿Estás loco, o qué te pasa? Do I look like Andrés Jackson to you?" When I just shrugged, wondering if he was some rich uncle I'd never heard of, she said, "What do you need twenty bucks for, anyway?"

I said the first thing that popped into my head. "For fireworks. We're doing a little thing back at school."

"Fireworks? You don't need money to watch no *stinkin'* fireworks! What are they gonna tell you, 'Don't look up'?"

Man, this lady was just impossible sometimes!

"But I want to light my *own*!" I shouted. "I'm a kid!

I'm supposed to be making memories! You never let me make any memories!"

"Memories?" she shot back. "*Pffft.* You're better off without them." Then her sharp eyes snapped down to my feet. "¡Y encima de todo, me estás ensuciando el piso! I just mopped and look at the mess you made!"

Fortunately, Patricio came in from the kitchen right then, because I wasn't getting anywhere with Paz.

"Hey, Grandpa, can I borrow twenty bucks?" I said.

My abuelo got a real serious look on his face. "Bueno, lo que digan mis deditos . . ."

So I stood there, like a total *menso*, watching as he raised both hands to his face, and then both pinky fingers to his ears, and then begin to wiggle them.

My grandpa gave a small shrug like, *What can I do? The pinkies have spoken.*

"¡Oye, toma!" snapped Paz.

I turned to see her digging a handful of change out of her pocket.

"Here," she said, dropping the coins in my hand. "Here's some money. Now go make some stupid memories and stop making a mess on my floors!"

CHAPTER 17

The local butcher shop up on Leyenda was about ten minutes from my grandparents' farm. It was a clean little hole-in-the-wall with a glass display case full of all kinds of tasty-looking cuts, and a string of salamis hanging on the back wall.

I considered buying one of the T-bone steaks in the display, but they were really expensive, and weren't even all that bloody looking.

No, what I needed to do was to sneak my way to the back, to where the *really* gross stuff happened— i.e., the chopping up of animal carcasses—in order to find a nice supply of that genuine ooey gooey. So I waited until the butcher dude got busy with a customer, and then slipped quickly under the counter and even quicklier (is that even a word?) through a swinging door.

Beyond the door was a hall that led into a large, well-lit room with a deep sink, a long stainless steel cutting table, a row of posters showing the various meaty cuts of farm animals (cow, sheep, pig, and goat), and a couple of big fridges.

I tried to think like a butcher—*What would I do with gallons and gallons of animal blood?*—and came up with two possibilities. Either a) trash it, or b) stick it in the fridge.

I decided option A was the more likely of the two, and had just started to tiptoe my way toward the nearest bin when someone said, "Uh, what are you doing back here?"

I whirled.

I gasped.

I choked.

My feet tangled, and I nearly *face-planted*!

Then, looking wildly around, I spotted the speaker.

And nearly face-planted *again*!

It was Liza! From school! She was sitting on the floor on the other side of the sink, her purple back-pack propped up behind her, a thick textbook open on her lap.

"Oh. Whoa! Hey! *Hi!*" I said, forcing my cheeriest smile to my lips.

She smiled back. Sort of. "Hi."

"Oh my gosh! Liza! *Hi!*"

Now her smile turned upside down. "Hi. Again."

"Hi!"

Yeah, my brain was apparently stuck on repeat.

I choked out a fake laugh. "Ha! Right. I'm just really big on introductions. But seriously, what are you doing back here?"

Liza frowned. "I'm pretty sure I asked you that first, but since our conversation seems to be having a little trouble achieving liftoff, I'll go. I'm doing homework. Pre-algebra equations, in case that was going to be the follow-up. Your turn."

"Uh, me too," I said, hardly knowing what to say.

Not surprisingly, she was now giving me the kind of look usually reserved for the person who ate your last cupcake. And I couldn't exactly blame her.

"Well, not *that* kind of homework," I said, really grasping at straws here. "Not school stuff. What I mean is, my grandma sent me out, uh, grocery shopping."

"Okay, but all the groceries are out front, so what are you doing sneaking around *the back*?"

Uh . . . uh . . . "B-b-because the butcher looked kind of busy."

"Hmm. So maybe it's different in L.A., but here people usually just do this really weird thing called 'waiting in line' when that happens."

"Ha. Yeah. No. Not in L.A.," I said, trying to play it all cool. "In L.A., we're all about self-serve. In fact, we've even been known to butcher our own meat!"

Liza was still staring, probably trying to decide whether I was kidding or not. And whether she was talking to a lunatic or not.

I smiled.

Liza didn't.

I went for a fist bump. She declined.

I began to sweat. Then something hit me. "Hold up," I said. "I thought you were vegan or something."

"I am vegan or something."

"Then what are you doing in a butcher shop?"

"My homework. Remember?" Seeing my somewhat confused look, she leaned forward to whisper, "Actually, I'm just pretending to do homework. What I'm *really* going to do is hide out back here until they close, then I'm going to liberate all the butchered animal meat in this place and dump it in the parking lot out front. It's my latest form of protest. Want to help?" Seeing my even more confused (and quite possibly terrified) look, she laughed and said, "I'm just messing with you, Jorge. It's my dad's shop. I usually hang out back here until he closes up."

"Oh, wow. Okay." That was a relief. "Wait. So . . . *your* dad is the town butcher?"

"Pretty ironic, I know. A hardened animal rights activist born to a third-generation butcher. I guess fate really does have a sense of humor, huh?"

"Guess so . . ."

She gave a little shrug. "Yeah, I don't condone what my father does for a living, but at least I've convinced him to only sell the meat of animals that were treated humanely. That is, up until the point they were slaughtered, of course."

"Definitely a step in the right direction," I agreed. Because what do you even say to something like that?

Closing her math book, Liza pushed to her feet. "Anyway, since you're obviously in a hurry, I'll help you out. What did your grandma want you to buy?"

"Sangre."

"Sangre?"

"Uh, yeah! You know, blood?"

Liza frowned. "She sent you out to buy *blood*?"

"Uh-huh. Good ole vein juice. Or as I like to say, 'the tomato sauce of life'!" Yep, I was babbling again . . .

Her frown deepened. "I don't think we're even allowed to sell that."

"Aw, man, seriously?"

"Or maybe it's just that no one's ever come in asking for it. What's your grandmother trying to make, anyway?"

"She's, um ... trying to ... to make some ..." Then, like a lightning bolt from heaven, it came to me. "Blood sausages!"

Yup, I'm pretty good at coming up with stuff in a bind.

Liza blinked.

"See, my grandma's part English," I lied. "On her, uh, Mexican father's mother's great-goddaughter's side."

Liza blinked again. "Oh. Well, I think my dad keeps the bags of blood in the walk-in."

"Awesome! I'll take two, please!" I dug into my pocket and brought out my stash of moolah. Okay, my five *measly* quarters. "Can we pretend these are Bitcoin?" I said, but Liza was already shaking her head.

"Don't worry about it. I'm not going to charge you. My dad always just trashes it, anyway."

"¡No manches! For real? Hey, I definitely owe you one."

"I'll remember that," she said teasingly, and then started toward the big stainless steel fridge with me trailing behind. "I'm just glad your grandma has a use for it. It seems pretty wasteful to throw away all that blood all the time." She paused, glancing back at me with a small smile tugging at the corners of her mouth. "Want to hear something funny?"

"Sure."

"When you first asked for the blood, you were acting so strange that the only thing I could think of was that you were secretly trying to hunt down some grub for your pet chupacabra or something . . ."

CHAPTER 18

Feeding a chupacabra is scary business.

I learned that the hard way. One second, Carter was staring hungrily up at me like some baby bird waiting for its mommy to puke-feed it some grubs or whatever. The next second, great white fangs flashed in the dark. Then—*WHAM!*—the seven-foot-tall mosquito attacked the bag o' blood like he was afraid it might grow a pair of furry legs and run away.

His jaw worked.

His lips slurped.

The hundred muscles of his throat wiggled and flexed as his teeth sank deeply into the crinkly plastic.

Meanwhile, I was totally

glued to the spot. I couldn't move. Couldn't even blink! I was fascinated! I was *terrified*! It was like watching a wild animal attack its prey in Nat Geo—only, even more savage somehow!

In less than five seconds flat, the dude had slurped exactly three XL Slurpees' worth of blood, and hadn't even paused to take a breath!

As his dark blue tongue lapped up the last of the sangre, Carter asked, "Did I get any on my face?"

Then we just sat there for a while, both of us staring down at the empty, shriveled-up bag in his giant, clawed hand.

At last I said, "Hey, I've been wondering. Are there *more* like you?"

"There were."

"Really?"

"Yeah, a loooong time ago. The largest chupacabra kingdom in the entire world was jess a few miles north of here, in those wild woods."

"Seriously?"

"Uh-huh. We lived in peaceful harmony with both nature and beast until one day the chupadedos—that's you all—turned on us and began huntin' us for our lovely coats and most beautiful fangs. They herded us up like sheep and whipped us like donkeys and then slaughtered us like vacas! And now," he said solemnly, "now . . . I'm all that's left."

"You mean they wiped out your entire *species*?" I burst out. Man, that was like premeditated extinction! It was . . . I don't know. Just plain *WRONG!*

Carter showed off his fangs again. "Nah, I'm just messin'! There's a buncha chupacabras! Estamos en todas partes. Pretty much anywhere you find goats."

"So, you have, like, a family, then?" I asked.

"Yeah."

"Nearby?"

"Well, *somewhere* . . ."

"What do you mean, 'somewhere'?"

He gave a sad little shrug. "No sé dónde están."

"You mean, *they're lost*?"

"More like *I'm* lost. For almost a week now. I can't find them."

"You're not messing with me again, are you?"

Carter shook his furry head, and his bat ears twitched and hung down sorta gloomily.

"So what are you going to do?"

"What *can* I do? I have to keep lookin' for them. And stay nearby . . . Hope my mother is lookin' for *me*."

"And your family isn't at your house . . . *er*, tree, or whatever?"

"We don't live 'round here," he said. "We don't live 'round *any*where, really."

"So you're migratory animals?"

"No, we jess move from place to place accordin' to the seasons."

I let that one slide.

Carter added, "Also accordin' to how quickly the farmers realize we're suckin' on their livestock."

"Wouldn't want to overstay your welcome, huh?"

"Oh, we never welcome."

I bet, I thought. Then, noticing that the chupacabra was looking a little down and a little lonely, I said, "I know what that's like."

Which surprised him. His big bright eyes fixed on mine. "¿Neta?"

"Oh, yeah. Well, the migrating part. Not the livestock-sucking part. My mom and me have been moving pretty much my entire life. Always changing neighborhoods, changing schools. Most of the time I barely even knew my own address."

"Did you move because of danger?"

"Nah, nothing like that. Just the regular stuff. Bills, finding work, money stuff. But it got me down, you know? I mean, it made me *mad*."

"Movin' made you mad?"

"Heck yeah! It sucks being the new kid in school every year. To be fair, though, it wasn't *just* the constant moving. I was mad because of other stuff, too."

"What stuff?"

I shrugged. "Stuff like my dad running out on us. He left when I was really little. And I got mad at my mom, too, because it didn't seem like she'd tried that hard to get him back."

"It was your mother's fault?"

"No. Things like that aren't anyone's fault, I don't think. But it still made me mad." I huffed out a sad chuckle. "Honestly? I was mad pretty much all the time."

Carter watched me for a few seconds, his long skinny tail swinging back and forth like the pendulum on a grandfather clock. Finally, he asked, "You still mad?"

My shoulders went up and down again. "I guess."

"Why?"

"Lots of stuff."

"Same stuff?"

"Same stuff . . . new stuff . . . just *stuff.*" I shook my head. I really didn't want to talk about it. But Carter kept staring at me. Staring and waiting, like now that I'd brought it up, I had to dish. And I guess I just had so much pent-up frustration about everything that I finally *popped.*

"Well, for one, I *hate* it out here, okay? This place stinks!"

The chupacabra looked totally confused. His blue eye was big and surprised looking, his green one small and curious. "You hate it?"

"Dude, how can I not? The only reason I'm even here is because my mom basically kicked me out of my own house! She *dumped* me here! And now I'm a billion miles from home!"

Outside, the wind swirled around the toolshed.

The door creaked. The sagging roof groaned.

We sat there in silence until Carter said, "We chupacabras don't believe home is a place. For us, it's not a somewhere. We believe home is *a feelin'.*"

Shaking my head, I stared unseeingly down at my sneakers as anger burned like a hot knot in my stomach. "Yeah, well, that's easy for you to say," I grumbled. "You can just pick any old tree in the forest. But that's not how people live. That's not how we're *supposed* to live."

And suddenly, I was crying. I didn't know why. The tears just came.

"What's wrong?" whispered Carter.

"Bro, don't you get it?" I said. "My own *mom* ditched me! She left me and she doesn't even care that she left me, because she probably never even loved me in the first place!"

The stupid waterworks were really pouring down my face now, and I felt completely ridiculous sitting there. Like a complete goof, in fact.

I mean, here I was, bawling my eyes out in front of Chewbacca's goat-slurping cousin! Talk about epically embarrassing.

There was another short silence. The wind blew

harder. The door creaked louder. At last, Carter said, "Just because someone leaves you doesn't mean they don't love you. Sometimes they leave *because* they love you. To *protect* you."

That stopped me.

It stopped me cold. I blinked the tears out of my eyes, and for a few seconds I just sat there, thinking.

For some reason, his words had struck a nerve. They really had. And maybe it was because I'd never actually thought about it that way.

See, in my mind, when someone leaves, it's like they're running away from whoever they're leaving. Trying to get away from the problem.

But what if that wasn't always the case? What if Carter was right? What if sometimes people left for the good of the *other* person? Not to ditch them, but to *help* them. To keep their loved one from getting tangled up in a messy situation or whatever?

And what if that's exactly what *my* mom was trying to do for me? Not sending me out here as punishment, but to give me a more . . . *stable* life, maybe.

She was always talking about how important it was for me to have stability. And with all the moving around we had to do, I didn't have much of it.

Wiping my face, I looked up at the chupacabra. He was sitting perfectly still, but his pointy ears were twitching like a couple of furry satellite dishes trying to catch a signal. "Man, you can get kind of deep for a bloodsucker, huh?"

Carter shrugged. "Uh-huh. 'Specially when I dig in for the night."

"That's not what I'm—"

The explosion of coppery-scented gas that came out of that three-hundred-pound, Yao Ming–height bloodivore was so shocking, and the smell so awful, and the sound so ridiculously *GINORMOUS*, that I couldn't help but bust out laughing.

"Dude! *PEEEE-YEW!*" I shouted, swiping at the air in front of my nose. "Let a brother know when you're going to bless us with your inner essence!" Heck, his *outer* essence was already a noseful!

"Sorry," Carter said with an embarrassed grin. "But that was some *tasty* blood."

CHAPTER 19

The next morning, I got up super early—I'm talking *cock-a-doodle-doo* early—and hustled out to the toolshed to check up on Carter.

But the second I stepped inside and saw the empty lawn chair, I knew he was gone. And my heart pretty much sank to my toes.

It was weird, I know. Feeling that way about a chupacabra of all things . . . I mean, it wasn't like Carter was some cute little puppy I'd found on the side of the road or something. (Though technically I *had* found him by the side of the road.) The dude was basically a giant mosquito. A mosquito with *fangs*!

Still, he was a pretty cool guy. Or creature. Whatever. And I don't know . . . I guess I'd been hoping we'd get to hang out some more.

Feeling a little lousy—and a lotta lonely—I started

back toward the house, kicking rocks as I went. I'd just lined up a nice big one with the toe of my sneaker when I heard someone shout my name.

I turned. Maybe two baseball diamonds away, from inside the thick trees on the southwest edge of my grandparents' farm, something was waving at me. Something big and brown and furry.

My first thought was *What the—?*

But my second was *Carter!*

I didn't think; just raced over to the lovable sangre-slurper. And the moment we were both hidden in the trees, I said, "Bro, I thought you'd ditched me!"

"Nah." He grinned, his curly brown fur blowing in the breeze. "I jess had to fertilize some shrubs. They looked like they were feeling un poquito sickly."

Just then, the wind changed direction, blowing this way now—and all of a sudden, I got a whiff of his "fertilizing."

Honestly, I was just happy he hadn't "fertilized" the toolshed. *Geesh!*

Carter's eyes sparkled. His fangs gleamed in the early morning sunshine.

"You're looking better," I said.

"I'm feelin' better."

Now I'm feeling un poquito sickly.

"So, uh, what are you going to do for the rest of the day? Just chill in the woods? Hope your family comes to find you?"

The chupacabra's long, kangaroo-shaped head went up and down like, *Yeah, I guess.*

Suddenly, an idea struck me. "Hey, I don't have any school today, and it's a long weekend, so if you want some company, maybe we can, um, hang out?"

Carter blinked. "You mean, upside down? From branches?"

"No, I mean, like, *play.* Have fun. Do chupacabras like to have fun?"

I know, I know. It was a totally ridiculous question. And a totally ridiculous visual, too. Can you imagine a bunch of giant bloodsuckers running around the woods, playing duck, duck, goose or something? *¡Híjole!* But from the way his eyes lit up and his batty ears twitched and those thin furry lips of his pulled back to show about a ruler's worth of shiny, smiling fangs, I knew I had my answer.

CHAPTER 20

Making friends is a funny thing. You never know when or where it's going to happen, or even *how* it happens. But when it does, it's usually one of those forever things.

After that morning, Carter and I were practically inseparable, kinda like chips and guac. We did everything together.

We played hide-and-seek.

We played pin the fangs on the goat.

We climbed trees.

Well, Carter climbed trees. I mostly just held on for dear life.

We drank slushies from the local 7-Eleven (blood-red raspberry flavor, of course).

We told each other our deepest secrets.

And we even went exploring in the woods, on what Carter called "treasure hunts."

Sometimes we'd just hang out on the roof, waiting for the moon to come up. Carter loved moon-watching, too. He said it reminded him of his mom.

Silly as it might've sounded, I had as much fun hanging out with that overgrown mosquito as I'd had with anyone. *Ever.*

And I even learned all sorts of interesting facts about chupacabras.

Fact #1: Chupacabras burrow and sleep underground, like woodchucks!

Fact #2: A full-grown chupacabra can stand over ten feet tall and weigh over *five hundred* pounds!

Fact #3: A chupacabra's fur can change color, chameleon style, to help them blend into different habitats!

Fact #4: Chupacabra saliva contains a natural anesthetic, which supposedly makes their prey feel soothed and totally chillaxed while the chupacabra is feeding.

But one of the funniest things about Carter: he was just as interested in my regular everyday life as I was in his.

So I told him everything I could think of. I told him about Pemberly and about my teachers and all about the different subjects I was taking. I told him about my two awesome new friends, Ernie and Liza, and about the not-so-awesome bully *losers*, Zane and his gang of zonzos. I told him how frustrated I was that Ernie was still getting picked on and that no one seemed to care, and Carter offered me some, well, *interesting* advice.

Carter was also super curious about my life back home, so I told him all about L.A., too, and all the times I'd gotten into trouble at my old school.

But the coolest thing about Carter? He never judged me. In fact, he was the one person—er, *thing*—who knew what it felt like to be me. Who knew exactly what it was like to have people judge you by all the outside stuff, like the color of your skin—in my case—or the size of your fangs—in Carter's.

He explained how chupacabras were totally misunderstood and were always getting blamed for all sorts of things they didn't actually do.

Story of my life, by the way.

According to him, chupacabras were sustainable hunters. Meaning they rarely ever killed the animals they fed on. Just like their mini-me's, mosquitos.

But since no one really gave chupacabras a fair shake and just judged them by everything they'd heard, or had seen, or thought they'd seen, Carter had grown up thinking of himself as a monster, because that's how the world saw him.

The funny part was, I'd always seen myself as a troublemaker because that's how I felt the world saw *me*. I guess the thing we both needed to learn was to stop living up to other people's expectations, and start living up to our own.

Anyway, as the days passed, we began rubbing off on each other, the way best friends tend to do. Hanging out with someone as chill and as easygoing as Carter made me feel . . . I don't know. Less *upset*, I guess. Less frustrated with stuff. I noticed how he never took anything too seriously, that classic "qué será, será" attitude, and always found the beauty in things. Especially in nature. He loved the smell of trees and the soft, crumbly feel of earth under his big padded feet, and the sounds of the wild—chirping crickets, singing birds.

On the flip side, hanging out with me helped Carter learn to think things through a bit more. Y'know, control those wild, animal impulses of his. After a while he stopped mindlessly chasing squirrels into thorny bushes and cannon-balling into shallow ponds.

We were such big influences on

each other that before long, Carter started using straws (yeah, seriously), and I found myself starting to appreciate nature (yeah, seriously).

As a matter of fact, pretty soon, the only thing I really missed from home—besides my mom, of course—was baseball. And so I did the only sensible thing. I taught the chupacabra how to play.

BASEBALL 101 FOR BLOODSUCKERS

It was going okayish . . .

Maybe he was teething?

Once he finally got the swing of things (no pun intended), the guy was a total animal! (Pun totally intended.)

Just two hours into his first lesson, he smashed such a moon shot that we didn't see it land. We didn't even *hear* it!

Unfortunately, though, that turned out to be the last pitch of the day. Because unfortunately, that's when things took a detour into *Deadlyville*.

It was a couple minutes past seven, with the sun already setting behind the tops of the faraway trees.

We were wandering through the woods in search of Carter's home run ball when we found something else—something *horrible*.

Only at first, I didn't really get it. I thought I was looking at a field of sleeping, half-starved cows.

But when I saw the jutting bones and the bulging, bloodshot eyes, and smelled an oh-so-puke-inducing stench, and heard the buzz of ten thousand swarming flies, I finally understood.

Those weren't sleeping cows.

Those were—

SLAUGHTERED COWS !!!

CHAPTER 21

Carter began to hiss. A low, threatening sound, like the warning of an angry cat. I watched his ears flatten back against the big dome of his head, and his curly fur bristle like the spines of a porcupine. Then he was moving, creeping toward the massacre without saying a word. And I realized I was moving with him, without saying anything, either.

Even from almost a baseball field away, I could make out huge fang-like marks on the cows' shriveled necks, and huge clawlike slashes on their sunken sides.

And my mouth simply spoke the words that were screaming through my brain. "Dude, did . . . *chupacabras* do this?"

"No," whispered Carter. "A chupacabra would

never treat any animal like dis. Dis . . . dis was done by *guachapos*."

Suddenly, there was a loud *squish!* and I felt my feet sink into the ground. The ground that I realized was soaked with—ugh, GROSS!—some kind of liquid nasty! Blood or guts or probably *bloody guts*!

I stumbled backward and—*SLURRRP!*—my right sneaker was sucked right off my foot! I watched it sink slowly into the bubbly goop, like some heroic but fatally wounded battleship.

Then the stench of the stuff—of the *entire* field, really—washed over us, enveloping me like the world's clingiest stink bomb, and it was all I could do not to refund last night's arroz con pollo.

"Want me to get your shoe?" asked Carter.

I shook my head. "Nah, forget it." I wouldn't have put that back on even if Converse signed me to a sneaker deal. When I finally couldn't look at the cows anymore, I said, "Dude, what are guachapos?"

The chupacabra didn't answer. Not right away, at least. He just stood there, sampling the air through the flared arches of his muzzle-y nose.

At last he said, "They . . . they're supernatural vampire dogs."

"*Supernatural vampire dogs?* ¡No manches! I mean, you're kidding, right?" And just when I was starting to like this place, too!

"Neta, neta. They're *true* monstruos. Vicious. Soulless. Your kind calls dem 'dips.' They're nature's most deadly predators."

Man . . . and I used to think regular old pit bulls were scary!

"They're the reason I got separated from mi familia," Carter said tightly.

"Seriously?"

"They attacked us a few nights ago. The night we first met. I was hidin' from dem. Up in your grandmother's tree."

Qué barbaridad. But that made perfect sense, didn't it? I remember how sad he'd sounded. How scared. How alone.

"So those things live around here?"

Carter shook his head. "No. Guachapos no viven anywhere. They always on the move. They live only for the thrill of the hunt. And what they love to hunt most of all is *chupacabras*."

Oh, wow. That didn't sound so good. "But—but how come I've never heard of these things? I mean, I used to watch *Animal Planet* all the time."

"You probably *have* heard of dem!" said Carter. "Only in scary stories. In old leyendas. Like chupacabras, dips are rarely ever seen, so few people believe they exist. Pero they as real as I am. 'Cept a whole lot meaner."

You can say that again, I thought, looking back at those poor cows. "So what's the plan?"

The chupacabra blinked, a big owl-like blink. "¿Qué plan?"

"What d'ya mean, *¿qué plan*? We gotta tell someone about these things, no? The cops. Animal control. The Avengers! *Somebody!*"

"If you tell, no one believe you," Carter said. "If I tell, maybe they believe, but they'll also probably try to *kill* me." His furry face was tense with worry. "Besides, your kind cannot fight these monstruos.

Cages cannot hold dem, and your weapons cannot hurt dem."

"So what do we do, then?"

Carter looked gravely at me as he said, "Only one thing we can do. Pray dey already moved on."

CHAPTER 22

The field of vamp'd cows was without a doubt one of the scariest things I had ever seen. In my entire *life*.

But eventually, when we were far, *far* away from that place and I could no longer smell that rotting stink on my clothes, or see that awful, bloodcurdling scene of a hundred and one slain bovines, I started to relax a little.

Then, just like Carter had said, I prayed. Prayed that those things had left, that they'd moved on. That they'd made like Tostitos Scoops and *dipped*.

Because if I never ever *ever EVER* saw something like that again, it would still be too soon.

Sunday night, my mom called. We talked for a little bit, and she asked me all about how things were going—how I liked New Mexico, and how the kids at school were treating me.

I said everything was cool, but that I missed hanging out with her and sneaking spoonfuls of her tres leches cakes (my mom was an awesome chef), and that got her all choked up. I could hear it in her voice as she started apologizing for sending me out here and all that, and explaining how important she thought it was for me to have some kind of consistency in my life.

I told her to forget it, that I was fine. Which surprised her. But it also surprised *me*.

I guess I just wasn't so sour about the whole thing anymore. I really wasn't. And Carter—who I obviously couldn't talk about—was a big reason for that.

Anyway, she made me promise that I wasn't mad and that I still loved her, and I made her promise to come visit soon, and she said she would.

It was great to hear her voice.

That Monday there was no school, so Ernie and Liza came over to work on our wardrobe assignment for the upcoming play.

Surprisingly, the project turned out to be pretty

dope. It didn't take long for me to get the hang of a sewing needle, and we mostly just sat around cutting and sewing and laughing at each other's dumb jokes. Ernie had brought along a grocery bag's worth of yummaliciousness (Baby Ruth and Mars bars, Snickers and Skittles), which kept our taste buds busy and our bodies nicely alimentados. Honestly, it was turning out to be the perfect Monday. You know, nice and chill.

That is, until another buddy of mine decided he wanted in on the fun.

Liza, Ernie, and I were sitting on the floor in the middle of my room, and through the window behind them, I saw Carter's smiling, fang-lined face rise slowly into view.

Only his smile didn't last long.

It quickly turned upside down and he started waving at me real urgently, like he desperately needed to talk.

I mouthed the words, *One sec! Be right out!*

But apparently that was one sec too long for the impatient, fur-covered *beanpole*, because he ignored me and, silently inching open my window, began to climb in! Liza and Ernie, for their part, were totally oblivious to the encroaching cryptid while I, on the other hand, was totally panicking!

When he was about halfway through, one of Carter's bony elbows bumped my baseball trophy on the nightstand. The big golden mitt began to wobble . . . and wobble . . . and wobble . . .

And panicking like a chicken in Colonel Sanders's kitchen, I did the only thing I could think of.

I leapt to my feet and raced over to the other side of the room—the side *opposite* the window—pointing up at this big ugly stain on the wall.

"Hey, check it out!" I shouted.

"Uh, what are we supposed to be checking out?" asked Liza.

"I-it's my favorite stain in the room!" I was doing my best impersonation of a frenzied chimp, jumping up and down and gesturing wildly with both hands, trying to keep their eyes on me and off the *seven-foot-tall bloodsucking monster* climbing in through my bedroom window. "Actually, it's my favorite in the whole house!"

Ernie frowned. It was a really sad-looking one, too. "You have a favorite stain . . . ?"

"¿Cómo no, chico? Who doesn't?" I scoffed. "And if you squint your eyes just right, it looks exactly like Selena Gomez!"

"Uh, no it doesn't," Liza said, squinting.

"Sort of?"

"Nope," said Ernie, also squinting.

"Kind of?"

"Negative," replied Liza.

"Just a little from the side, maybe?" I tried.

"*No*," they both said firmly.

Now, did they think I'd gone totally loco? Probably. But did I care? Nope.

See, while they'd been busy staring at the stain, squinting their eyes and twisting their heads trying to see Selena, I'd been frantically—and *sneakily*—shooing Carter toward the closet.

And FINALLY he got the message. Dracula's furry second cousin tiptoed his way between the doors, quiet as a mouse, and shut himself inside.

And the moment he did, relief swelled up in me like a tsunami. Only the wave never came anywhere near reaching its crest, because just then, from inside the closet, there came a huge *CRASH!*

Ernie's head whipped toward the sound. *"What was that?"*

Me on the outside

What? I didn't hear anything.

Me on the inside

WHAT IN THE FRIJOLES WAS CARTER DOING IN THERE?

Another tumble of boxes—some banging, too.

"Oh, *that!* That's ... that's nothing," I said. "Me and my grandma, we, uh, like to play closet Jenga with old suitcases and shoeboxes. And sometimes when the stack gets really dicey, we leave it alone for a day or two to see if someone wins. And it sounds like that's one point for *this guy*!" I flashed them my cheesiest grin, giving myself the classic two-thumb salute.

Unfortunately, neither one seemed to be buying it. And to make things even *worse*, just then, there was another crash of boxes, and this time we all clearly heard, "OWWW!"

"And what was *that*?" shouted Liza.

¡Santo cielos! "Oh, probably the rats," I blurted. "There's a family of them in there." Another *crash!*, and I added, "An *extended* family. You know how quickly rats breed."

"Dude, that didn't sound like any rats I've ever heard," said Ernie, picking up his collectable Star Trek phaser pen and aiming the business end at the closet doors like he could actually zap someone with it.

"Oh, c'mon, E-dog! What else could it've been?" I said. "Don't tell me you still believe that monsters live in closets!"

Ernie, however, was looking at me like maybe he still *did* believe it. And in this very special case, he wasn't so wrong.

"Jorge, that wasn't rats," said Liza, eyes locked on the closet. "There's someone in there!"

Yep, *BUUUSSSTED!*

Darting past them, I put my hands out in a *just chill* gesture and pressed my back flat against the doors. "Yes, there *is* someone in there, okay? But I can only show you if you both promise, *promise*, PROMISE not to tell!"

"We promise," said Liza.

"Remember, what you see at Casa de Jorge *stays* at Casa de Jorge. It's kinda like Vegas that way."

"Jorge, we already promised. Now open that door, because I'm starting to get *really* worried about who you've got in there."

"All right, all right. But *relax*," I said. Then I took my own advice: I sucked in a deep, relaxing breath and eased open the closet doors.

And as the hairy, seven-foot-tall, sangre-sucking cryptid stepped slowly, shyly into view, I said, "World, meet Carter."

CHAPTER 23

"I fight for animal rights!" screamed Liza, snatching up my baseball-bat lamp and raising it threateningly. "Please don't make me hurt you!"

"Put that down!" I whisper-shouted. "You're going to scare him!"

"Scare him?" Liza shot back. "He's scaring *me*!"

"Carter's harmless!" I said. "Well, unless you happen to be a goat, of course . . . then you're probably in trouble."

From the ceiling—and still upside down—Carter gave an embarrassed nod-shrug combo while I quickly crossed my room to shut the window. Explaining Carter to Ernie and Liza was already going to be a handful. I didn't need my grandparents, who were busy out by the chicken coop, to hear all the shouting and decide to join the party.

"I—I come in peace," said Ernie, raising one hand in the Vulcan V salute.

I smacked him on the arm. "Chico, put your hand down! He's a chupacabra, not E.T.!"

"So that's why you came to my dad's shop looking for blood," Liza whispered as it dawned on her. "You've been *feeding* that thing!"

The way she said it made it sound so bad, too. Like I'd been raising some evil baby monster in a tortoise tank like that kid from *Stranger Things*.

"Carter isn't a *thing*," I snapped. "He's my *friend*."

Liza's wide, frisbee-size eyes rose first to the frightened chupacabra who had come down from the ceiling and was now towering—er, *cowering*—behind me, then sank slowly back down to mine. She said, "Jorge, may I . . . have a word with you, *pretty please*?"

So the three of us gathered in the corner. The far corner. Farthest away from Carter, that is.

Liza rasped, "Have you lost your *mind*? How do you even know that thing?"

"We met a couple days ago . . . on the roof." I pointed.

"But how could you let a monster like that *in* the

house? That creature could *eat* you. Or me!"

"*Carter*," I corrected. "*Carter* could eat you."

"So you *AGREE*?"

"What? No, I don't agree. I'm just trying to tell you that Carter's not a *thing* or a *monster* or a *creature*— he's my buddy. And he's cool."

"So, how do you talk to him or whatever?" Ernie asked, glancing warily back at Carter.

"With my mouth," I said. "Duh. Carter, say hi!"

"I dance, too!" said Carter.

I grinned. "He does. I taught him la Macarena. Carter, show these gringos what's up, man!"

"That's *amazing!*" shouted Ernie.

"Gracias," Carter replied with a polite little bow.

Out of nowhere this big ole laugh just bubbled up out of Liza, sort of like a Mentos mint making a Coke volcano. "You taught him that?" she asked me.

"Yep," I said, nodding proudly. "He also plays guitarra. But he taught himself that."

"He's so tall," whispered Ernie, straight-up gawking now. "And so *terrifying!*"

I turned to Carter. "Try hunching down."

Carter slouched over, which somehow made him

look even creepier. "Does that help?" he asked.

"Not really," Ernie admitted.

Suddenly Liza's face paled. Her eyes got all big and scared again, and her lips got all tight and thin, as if she'd bitten into a freshly picked habanero.

Carter, looking a little worried himself now, said, "Want me to try squatting, maybe?"

But Liza wasn't listening to him. Her face was a mask of terror. "He's the monster . . ." she breathed, fumbling back a step. "It's *him!*"

"Don't you read the newspaper?" Liza asked me.

I shook my head. "People still read those?"

"Only people who care about the news!" she snapped. "Especially stories of bloodsucking cryptids slaughtering livestock all up and down an obscure little New Mexican town. A town by the name of *Boca Falls*!"

Ernie gasped. "That sounds like *our* obscure little town!"

"Dat wasn't me!" shouted Carter.

And I, of course, backed him up. "That definitely was not him!"

"How do you know?" asked Liza.

So I said, "Uh, you both might want to sit down for this . . ."

CHAPTER 24

After I'd given Ernie and Liza the 411 on the dips—aka the pack of vampiric nightmare dogs running around Boca Falls—they looked even more terrified than when they'd met Carter. I guess hearing about a bunch of roaming killer pooches can have that effect on you.

But thanks to Carter's goofy, fangy grin and his overall friendliness—not to mention his mad skills with a guitarra—eventually they both chillaxed. Especially after he played them his very own remix of the modern classic "Heaven" by Los Lonely Boys.

About an hour later, Ernie's mom called to say she was picking him up. He tried to negotiate for a little more time, but it's almost impossible to out-negotiate a mom. (Trust me, I know from experience.)

After I said goodbye to Ernie—and made him pinky swear to keep Carter our "little" secret—Liza figured it was time for her to start heading home, too.

I decided to leave Carter at the house and walk with her, because a) it was still light out and we couldn't risk him being spotted, and b) walking and talking with a friend would give her a chance to wrap her head around the fact that she'd just met a real-life chupacabra.

Overall, she seemed to be taking the whole thing pretty well. In fact, she was taking things *so* well that she was already talking about using Carter as her muse—her inspiration to take our chupacabra costume to the next level.

Liza was super cool, though. And since she was a huge animal lover and understood the kind of danger we would put Carter in by telling anyone about him, I knew that I didn't have to make her swear any kind of phalangeal oath, pinkies or otherwise.

Liza lived way closer than Ernie, who lived almost thirty minutes away, in one of the fancy neighborhoods. And as we walked, she asked me all sorts of questions about Carter.

It wasn't until I was on my way back from Liza's, walking by myself along a sleepy little back-country road on the south side of town, that I wished we hadn't just been talking about Carter—that we'd actually brought him along.

Because that's when things got ... well, *sketchy*.

CHAPTER 25

I'd just reached the "busy" intersection by the town's little strip mall (not a car, moped, or even a horse-pulled *buggy* anywhere in sight), when I heard a high-pitched whistle.

Next came several loud barks of laughter, and I turned to see a bunch of kids on shiny chrome bikes riding this way.

They began calling to me, like they knew me or something. And then I realized—¡Santo cielos!—they did know me. It was Zane and his gang of soccer burros from school!

The looks on their vicious, grinning, sweaty faces told me exactly what they were thinking.

But just in case I couldn't tell, one of them decided to translate for me. "You better start running, *spudz!*"

Now, I'm a proud Chicano. Proud to the power of *P*. As a matter of fact, my roots probably trace all the way back to the bravest Aztec warriors in all of pre-Colombian Mexico.

That being said, I wasn't too proud to run!

I took off down the middle of the empty street with sweat already rolling down my face and a stitch already forming in my side.

I didn't want to turn around. I didn't want to look back. But I couldn't help it! And when I finally did, I didn't like what I saw. Zane and his circus of brainless jock-clowns were up out of their seats, pumping their pedals wildly as they zoomed straight for me.

Yep. Time to summon my inner Sonic. (That's Sonic the Hedgehog, for you non-gamers out there.) Gritting my teeth, I ran harder, faster. But it wasn't enough. The vibrating hum of their wheels only grew louder and louder! My heart thundered in my chest. Their laughter thundered in my ears. Panic lodged halfway down my throat, like LA's *Levitated Mass* boulder sculpture.

Desperate, I looked around for a grocery store or fire station—any place I could run into for help. Back home, there was one every other block. Out here, there didn't seem to be one for another thousand *miles*!

Up ahead the road curved slowly east, in the direction of my grandparents' farm. And that's when it finally hit me.

There was just no way.

Zero chance I could outrun these punks!

No! Shut up, me! DON'T GIVE UP!

Off to my left, acres and acres of high grass rolled all the way out to the horizon like a swaying green carpet.

There was no time to think deep or long, so I just thought fast: I put on a wild burst of speed, plunging face-first into the grass!

My idea was simple: bikes were made for streets and sidewalks, not divots and hills and rocky earth. So if I took our little high-stakes game of tag off-road, I might be able to take away most of their speed advantage.

They probably wouldn't even follow me in, I told myself. *Even they're not that boneheaded!*

I was wrong. They were that boneheaded.

They burst into the grass after me like a gang of bloodthirsty lawn mower racers.

Their laughing, shouting voices filled the air, and the sound of their wheels crunching and crackling over the tall weedy stalks grew louder and sharper, until a foot-shaped flash of pain suddenly lit up my left butt cheek.

The force of the impact knocked me off-balance, and as I pitched forward, I had time to think, *¡Me patearon!*

Then I face-planted. *Hard.*

And the punks swarmed.

CHAPTER 26

I heard a voice say, "Nice kick, Jay!"

And another, "Excellent footwork, Mr. Pendleton!"

Then tires and sneakers were crowding all around me. Hands were reaching for me. They picked me up, and held me up, and shoved me back and forth between other hands that grabbed and slapped and poked at me.

Okay, maybe not totally fine . . .
I mean, there were a LOT of them!

But I was no gallina. Being surrounded by a bunch of bullying dill weeds didn't scare me. I was totally fine.

"Well, lookie, lookie what the trashman dragged in," said Zane, grinning a pimply, red-faced grin.

"I think you're confusing your clichés there, sport," I pointed out.

But did he appreciate my helpfulness? Nope. Instead he just lifted his meaty leg and—*wham!*—full-on kneed me in the stomach.

"And I think you got a big mouth," I heard him say as I doubled over, my eyeballs trying to pop out of my face.

Somehow I managed to gasp, "Yeah, it's definitely plus size."

Zane stooped so he could whisper directly into my ear, and his breath was hot against my cheek. "A little birdie told me you tried to rat me out to Skennyrd," he said. "Want to apologize, *ese*?"

"Hey, man, I might be a Mexi*can*," I said, "but that's just something I *can't* do." And before I could stop it, my traitor mouth added, "Especially not with your stanky breath all up in my face. Seriously. Would popping an Altoid really kill you?"

Yeah, definitely not the kind of thing you want to

say when trying to avoid a beating. And in case you were wondering, I was *totally* trying to avoid a beating.

Anyway, you guessed it. *Wham!* Another knee to the gut.

This one made me want to puke. And not just my lunch, either . . . all my guts and vital organs, too.

When I'd finally caught my breath again (and the world had stopped seesawing around me for half a second), I said, "Y'all think I'm scared of you punks? I'm from L.A., okay? I wrap dummies like you up in some jamoncito and eat you with my breakfast tortillas!"

A big mocking "*OOOOOOOHHHH!*" came from the assembled dummies.

Then the chief dummy said, "Oh, yeah? Well, here's a little appetizer for ya, then!"

But as he reared back, preparing to force-feed me a knuckle sandwich (which, by the way, I didn't like half as much as breakfast tortillas), the strangest thing happened.

Or rather, the strangest *sounds* happened.

First came a spine-tingling rattling.

Then a bloodcurdling growling.

Then a stomach-clenching hissing that whispered eerily through the tall grass.

And every single person—and every single *eye* in every single *face*—first froze, then stared uneasily around in every single direction.

I had a second or two to think, *What was that?*

Then something huge and black and absolutely *TERRIFYING* sprang out of the grass with the hiss of a thousand snakes!

UN MONSTRUO!

Waaaaait . . . That wasn't no monstruo.

That was Carter!

CHAPTER 27

"Dude, you're like a superhero!" I told Carter as we started back home, strolling lazily along that dusty backcountry road. "A superhero with FANGS!"

The chupacabra grinned, his scrawny shadow seeming to stretch out ahead of us forever. "Nah," he said, shaking his head.

He just couldn't see it. So I broke it down for him like a fraction.

"Bro, check it: You're seven feet tall. You're sneakier than a senator. You have superhuman strength *and* superhuman speed. Face it, you're a *superhero*!"

Carter considered this. Then he shrugged. "Eh, maybe un poquito."

"You even got superhero timing!" I said. "I mean, did you see those guys? They were out for blood!"

The chupacabra's eyes bugged, cartoon style. "Those were *VAMPIRES*?!"

"What? No, I meant they were about to beat me up."

Carter blinked. "Oh."

As we reached the end of the street and crossed over, I noticed that the chupacabra's body language had taken a bit of a nosedive. His back was sort of slumped, and the worn-down heels of his Converse were sort of dragging along. His expression had changed, too. He looked about as cheerful as a thundercloud.

So I asked him what was up and he said, "I got something bad to tell you, Jorge. It's why I rushed over to your house earlier. But I didn't wanna say nothin' in front of tus amigos."

I didn't like the sound of that. "What is it? What's wrong?"

"There was another ataque."

"Another attack?"

"Another *slaughter*."

"You mean like that field of cows?"

Carter nodded gravely. "Ovejitas dis time. A

whole flock of sheep, less than ten miles from here."
Then his tone turned even grimmer. "The dips get-
tin' *closer* . . ."

I heard myself gulp. "What do you mean, they're
getting closer?"

"¿No entiendes? They're on my scent. They're
huntin' me!"

"Hunting you?"

"I tole you. Dips *hunt* chupacabras. Which
means . . ." He trailed off, looking lost. Heartbroken,
even.

"Which means what?"

His mismatched eyes rose sadly to meet mine.
"Which means I have to go."

Six little words. Just six. Still, they hurt more than
both of Zane's knees to the gut put together. Truth
was, I'd already had more than my share of people
leaving me. And I didn't think I could handle losing
my best friend, too. Not right now.

"'Go'?" I burst out. "Go where? What are you talking about?"

"Jorge, it's too dangerous . . . and not jess for me!
For your abuelitos. For *you*! The dips won't stop until
they find me. And meanwhile, they'll kill *anything*

they run into! Es lo que hacen. They kill with no mercy. No pity. They the reason everyone fears chupacabras. We get the blame for all they killin'. Those monstruos why we always on the move."

I didn't know what to think. I didn't know what to *say*. So I just blabbed the first thing that popped into my head. "But what if we ... we *stop* them, you know? Like in the movies! Yeah, what if we set up some kind of slick trap! That would be *sooo* sick!"

"Those things can't be trapped," Carter said ominously, and his fur darkened to match the dark tone of his voice. "I don't even know if they can be *killed*."

"What? Hold the guac. What do you mean, you 'don't even know if they can be killed'? In *Predator*, that big Schwarzenegger dude said if it bleeds, we can kill it!"

"Not these monstruos," he whispered. "They living *nightmares*. Creatures of leyendas. Not jess flesh and blood."

"So, how do the legends say you beat these things, then?"

"Bueno, when the old chupacabras—the elders— tell the stories, they always talk about how a kind act of the soul—like friendship, love, sacrifice—

is the only thing that can drive away evil."

"So, *what*? We're supposed to buy some puppy chow and throw these things a fiesta or something?"

"¡Eso es lo que quiero decir!" cried Carter. "I don't know *how* to stop them. And that's why I gotta leave!"

Around us, the wind sighed sadly through the trees. Rain clouds scuttled by. A cold gust blew in the first cold droplets and one splashed my cheek, running down my face like an icy tear.

I squeezed my eyes shut.

A loneliness had already begun to settle over me. Even though I wasn't alone. Not yet, anyway. And I *hated* that feeling. Though it was probably the most familiar one I knew . . .

"Where will you go?" I finally managed.

"Calle Hueso."

"Calle Hueso?"

"It's a small woodland area in northwestern Mexico. The oldest chupacabra enclave in the world. I think that's where mi familia went."

"How do you know?"

"I don't. But I can't find them, and they haven't found me, so I have to try." He paused, those frowning owl-like eyes studying my face. "Calle Hueso is a safe place for chupacabras. My mother probably expects me to meet her there. The only reason I haven't gone already is jess . . ." He trailed off again.

"Is *what*? Why haven't you gone?"

"Because I'm not sure I can make it. So much open country along the way. Nowhere to hide. And the dips are faster than me. *Much* faster."

"So you can't go, then. I mean, you can't risk your life!"

"I *have* to go," he said in a miserable tone. His pointy ears twitched uneasily. "I can't put you y tu familia in dis much danger. And I have to find *my* familia. I . . ." His head dropped, his eyes dropped, his heart seemed to drop. "I have to go to Calle Hueso."

Carter was determined to leave. I could tell. I'd had enough experience with people leaving me to be absolutely sure. And even though deep down inside I knew that him leaving *was* probably best for both of us, I couldn't just let him run off into danger and the unknown like that. What if the dips *did* run him down along the way? Or what if somebody spotted him? A hunter, like Skennyrd?

Just the idea of Carter's head mounted on someone's trophy wall got my insides all twisted up like a churro, and I said, "Look, just give me some time to figure out how to get you to Calle Hueso, okay? *Safely.*"

Carter started to shake his head, like he didn't want to hear it, but I had to *make* him hear it. I had to save my friend.

"Dos días," I said firmly. "That's all I'm asking for. Just give me two days!"

"Jorge—"

"Please! I just don't want to see you get hurt, okay? Honestly, I . . . I don't think I can handle that right now."

The chupacabra said nothing. Just watched me out of the corners of his sad eyes as we walked along, and I watched him out of the corners of mine.

Finally he said, "Okay. Dos días. But then I go."

CHAPTER 28

The next day at lunch, I told Liza and Ernie everything. How Carter wanted to go—*needed* to go—but how he'd never make it without our help. We all agreed about what had to be done, but none of us could figure out exactly *how* to do it.

"If only we had a matter-stream converter," Ernie said, sipping on his Coke and giving me the four-fingered Vulcan salute.

I crunched into a GMO-free, soy-free, corn-free, wheat-free, *flavor*-free chip that Liza had given me. "Or if we knew a Super Saiyan."

Liza ignored both of our insightful and totally realistic suggestions. "The question is," she wondered aloud, "how do we get a Shaq-size, bipedal vampire onto some kind of public transportation system without anyone noticing?"

A few ideas were running through my head . . .

But at the risk of sounding like a total tonto, I decided to keep them to myself.

Ernie sighed. "It'd be so much easier if Carter could just borrow one of our faces. You know, like they always do in the Mission Impossible movies?"

Liza stared at him like, *Seriously?*

Which is exactly how most people probably would have stared at him after a comment like that. But you had to give the guy mad props, because his words were like a lightning bolt to my brain!

Suddenly, I knew what to do.

"*¡ESO!*" I shouted, tossing a potato chip at Ernie. It bounced off his forehead, leaving an oily little smudge between his eyes. "Dude, that's *it*!"

He frowned. "Jorge, no. We don't have the equipment or the expertise to pull something like that off. Besides, whose face would we even use?"

"Bro, that's not what I'm saying."

"Then what *are* you saying?" asked Liza.

"What I'm saying is, what if Carter was someone else? No, better yet, what if he was some*thing* else entirely!"

"Well, now you're talking about full-on fairy godmother, magical metamorphosis," said Ernie. "Like the beast in *Beauty and the Beast*. Which, hate to burst your bubble, is going to be even *harder* to pull off."

The kid just didn't get it. Liza, on the other hand, could smell exactly what I was stepping in.

"He's not talking about metamorphosis," she said, her lips twitching upward into a grin. "He's talking about *Halloween*."

CHAPTER 29

You know how people say life is all about timing? Well, saving Carter's life looked like it was going to come down to exactly that.

See, Halloween was approximately three days away, and it just so happened to be the one time of year where you could dress up as a ghost, a goblin, a zombified tugboat captain, or even a two-headed unicorn, and not draw too much attention.

My plan was simple: throw a huge white sheet over Carter, cut him a pair of eyeholes, and put him on the first bus to Mexico.

But Ernie came up with an even better one. Instead of trying to *hide* Carter's "chupacabra-ness" (which was going to be pretty much impossible, anyway), the smartest move was to play it up! Let the chupacabra be a chupacabra.

In other words, hide Carter in plain sight!

Only—of course—make him look a little less *real* and a little more *costumey*.

Liza immediately went to work, embroidering Carter a baseball cap that read chupacabra and screen-printing him a T-shirt that said blood-etarian.

Meanwhile, Ernie and I got busy on a pair of sock-gloves to cover Carter's huge razor-sharp claws, since they looked a little too legit to be fake. We also bought him a new pair of sneakers—Converse size 21!—since that seemed to be his favorite brand, and to hide those gigantic, furry patas.

The next step was to solve the whole issue of smuggling/transporting a creature of legend.

With Mexico basically being a bajillion miles away, and none of us even having earned our learners' permits yet, much less our licenses, driving him ourselves was out of the question.

But the more we thought about it, the less we liked the idea of sticking Carter on some crowded bus. There were just way too many passengers. Too many hours on the road. Too many chances for someone to realize he wasn't in a costume.

A taxi didn't seem like such a hot idea, either. Taxi

drivers can be pretty chatty. Plus, they probably have a good eye for strange behavior, having spent so much time interacting with so many different people. Over the course of a sixteen-hour ride, Carter might start to stick out like a rainbow-colored piñata in a meat locker.

An airplane was just too dangerous. What if Carter had a panic attack forty thousand feet above sea level? Worse, what if some of the passengers realized what he was, and *they* all had panic attacks?

The only safe option (if you could even use the word "safe") seemed to be a train. One of those nice passenger trains where we could book Carter his own little cabin, and there wouldn't be any prying eyes or potential chatterboxes.

Fortunately, Ernie was able to find one that went from here all the way to Southern California, near Chula Vista. No, it wasn't *exactly* where Carter was heading. But it wasn't that far, either; and there were enough woods and preserves nearby to keep him nice and stealthified the rest of the way. Most importantly, it would give him almost a thousand-mile head start on the dips.

In the meantime, Liza drew up a lesson plan for me and Carter to work on. Basically, just some rules to memorize in case he needed to interact with anyone along his journey.

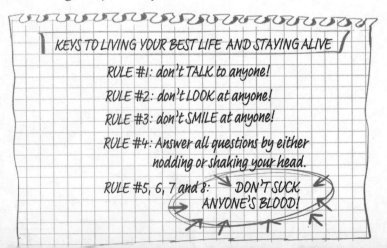

KEYS TO LIVING YOUR BEST LIFE AND STAYING ALIVE

RULE #1: don't TALK to anyone!

RULE #2: don't LOOK at anyone!

RULE #3: don't SMILE at anyone!

RULE #4: Answer all questions by either nodding or shaking your head.

RULE #5, 6, 7 and 8: DON'T SUCK ANYONE'S BLOOD!

* * *

That night found Carter and me in my room. We were going over the rules for about the zillionth time, running through some hypothetical situations, when we heard a knock on the front door.

It was a loud knock.

A *rude* knock.

The sort of knock that said, *If you don't open up, I'm just going to pound louder and harder until either you give in, or the door does.*

"Sounds like your abuelo's back from the grocery," whispered Carter, his furry tail twitching.

"Sounds like Paz," I said. Climbing off my bed, I told Carter to wait in the closet, then went out to the living room to let them in.

You know how when you were little, your mom told you to always ask who it is before opening the front door?

Yeah, well, it's a great tip. Because that way, when you *do* open the door, you won't be sorry who you opened it *to*.

Like I was now.

CHAPTER 30

"Principal Skennyrd," I breathed. "W-what are you doing here?"

"I was in the neighborhood." Ducking his head, he lumbered through the door like an ogre, shouldering me out of the way and splashing me with ice-cold rainwater. The dude felt like he'd been carved out of solid *rock*. It was like getting brushed aside by the Hulk. "Thanks for inviting me in," he said, even though I hadn't, and he sat down wetly on my grandparents' couch, even though I hadn't invited him to do that, either.

Beneath his Hagrid-esque heinie, the couch looked like it belonged in a doll house. Honestly, I was surprised it didn't crack down the center when he sat down.

Removing his floppy rain hat, Skennyrd said, "That's a rough storm out there."

I kept my eyes glued to him, but didn't say anything, and didn't dare sit down. This Chicano was nobody's fool. Principals didn't just randomly show up on your front porch in the middle of a thunderstorm. Something was up. Something *big*.

"Whatever happened," I said, "it wasn't me."

"But if you don't know what happened," said Skennyrd, "how do you know it wasn't you?"

"Because I haven't done anything. I've just been here."

Skennyrd's huge pale face twisted into a vicious grin. His sharp little teeth looked even smaller and sharper than usual. "Don't look so worried, Jorge. I'm not here because you're in trouble. I'm here because I need your help."

I almost choked on my surprise. "You need *my* help?"

"Strange, isn't it? Sometimes it's the people you think the least of in this world who come in the handiest."

Geez. Was the guy a black belt in the art

of the backhanded compliment or what?

"I've come to talk to you about one of your class-mates," Skennyrd went on. "A Jay Pendleton. Do you know him?"

I was pretty sure I'd heard the name. And I was pretty sure it belonged to the wannabe Cobra Kai prodigy who'd *hi-ya!*-kicked me in the heinie yester-day. I still had a bruise in the shape of a sneaker to prove it. Not that I was willing to show it to Skennyrd. "Isn't he one of Zane's amigos?"

"They're both on the soccer team, so I imagine he is."

"What does he have to do with me? I don't know him."

The couch groaned for mercy underneath Sken-nyrd as he leaned forward, meeting my gaze full-on. "Jay Pendleton and three of his cousins," he began slowly, "were violently attacked last night while play-ing in the woods eight or so miles north of here. Jay barely survived and is now in the hospital in critical condition."

Oh, man. "Critical condition?"

"That's right."

"Is he going to be okay?"

"The doctors are hopeful. But that's not why I'm here."

His eyes didn't leave mine, and I realized he was giving me a meaningful look. A look I didn't like. *At all.*

"Hold up. You don't think *I* had anything to do with that, do you?"

The not-so-friendly giant chuckled at that. "No, Jorge. See, Jay Pendleton was mauled by a wild animal. So unless you're quite a bit more ferocious than you look, or unless you have a pair of giant fangs hidden somewhere in that big mouth of yours, I think it's safe to assume it wasn't you."

And like a flash, it hit me. The dips! That pack of supernatural vampire dogs Carter was so scared of! It was them! They'd attacked Jay and his cousins!

Geez, those things are just as dangerous as Carter made them out to be . . . maybe even more!

Counting Jay, that made it three attacks now. Three attacks in the span of three days! And since those monstruos obviously didn't discriminate between anything with a heartbeat, all I could wonder was what or *who* was going to be next?

I tried to swallow the lump of fear in my throat as Skennyrd looked straight at me and said, "The attack occurred sometime between eight fifteen and nine oh five last night. And even though it was quite dark out, especially that deep in the woods, the other three children claim to have seen the creature that attacked Jay. Their descriptions are all wild and ridiculous sounding—yet *frighteningly* consistent." His rattlesnake gaze sharpened on mine. "They describe a creature—nay, a *monster*. One which you will not find in any taxonomical reference textbook. Trust me, I tried. But it's one that I believe *you* would be able to identify."

My eyes involuntarily flicked toward my bedroom. To where Carter was hiding. And I nearly blurted, "It wasn't him!"

But fortunately for me (and for Carter), I caught myself and, hoping my voice wouldn't give me away, instead said, "I—I don't know what you're talking about."

Skennyrd grinned. "Then maybe it's high time that I stopped talking and started *showing*," he said, setting his briefcase down on the coffee table. Thumbs as thick as salamis clicked open the locks and revealed what was inside. It was something I would have recognized anywhere . . . because up until I lost it in that muddy field, it belonged to *me*.

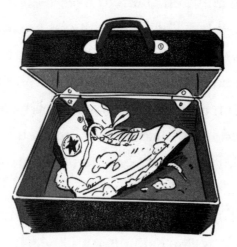

CHAPTER 31

For a moment, all I could do was stare at the sneaker, feeling like I was trapped in some nightmare, bizarro-world version of *Cinderella*. Not a glass slipper, but a blood-soaked sneaker. *My* blood-soaked sneaker!

Every single one of my fingers and toes had gone numb. Still, I tried to keep my expression perfectly natural as I watched Skennyrd fold back the tongue to reveal a name—*my name!*—scrawled sloppily across the tag.

The hunter's fingers closed slowly around the sneaker as he picked it up. In his enormous pale hand, it honestly looked like something straight out of babyGap. "Are you going to pretend it isn't yours?" he asked with an evil grin.

"Nah, it's mine," I admitted.

"Do you know where I found it?"

"No." A lie, obviously. But you always get one, right?

"I found it on Mr. Reuben's property, not too far from where Jay Pendleton was attacked. I found it in a field of cows. *Slaughtered* cows."

I heard myself swallow.

Skennyrd went on. "Mr. Reuben asked the sheriff and me to come down to take a look. But this is where it gets *real* interesante. See, it would stand to reason that if you happened upon such a spectacularly gruesome discovery, which you obviously did, you would have immediately reported it. At the very least you would have told some kids at school about it. But you didn't. You didn't tell a soul, did you?"

I exercised my right to remain silent, and Skennyrd continued: "And I know you didn't, because the first report regarding the cows came from Mr. Reuben himself, who discovered the massacre only recently. Which leads me to one very obvious conclusion: you, Jorge, are trying to protect someone . . . or, more precisely, some*thing*."

His massive upper body seemed to loom toward me and over me, even though he was sitting and hadn't actually moved. And his enormous shadow seemed to stretch over the entire room.

My heart was like an out-of-control jackhammer in my chest. I could hardly breathe.

"Now, granted, this would all be nothing more than mere speculation on my part," said Skennyrd, "except for one teeny, *tiny* little incident—our encounter that night on the road. When you tried to convince me that my eyes hadn't seen what they thought they'd seen, even though my eyes have never lied to me before." The pale square of his chin jutted out like a cinder block as he whispered, "You were trying to protect the creature then, and you're trying to protect it now, aren't you?"

My brain froze. Fear had risen up in my throat like vomit. I thought I was going to be sick. But instead of projectile puke, my mouth surprised me with "Are you feeling okay, Mr. Skennyrd? Do you want me to call a doctor or something? 'Cause you're not making much sense."

The world-class hunter grinned. It wasn't the friendly kind. "Don't play bobo with me, Jorge. There's a monster out there killing our livestock and mauling our boys, and I want you to tell me what it is and where I can find it, so that I can *kill it*."

I felt my insides turn to jelly. Those last two words had hit me like a sledgehammer to the gut. "The monster" Skennyrd was referring to was not only my best friend in the whole world, he was also less than twenty feet away, hiding in my room. And if Skennyrd's Spidey-senses started to tingle and he decided to search the place, there wouldn't be a thing in the world I could do to stop him.

Standing perfectly still, I tried to look all innocent, but I was pretty sure it wasn't working.

"You really think you can protect this thing, son?" Skennyrd said with a venomous chuckle. "Just in the last forty-eight hours alone, a flood of sightings and eyewitness reports have come pouring into the sheriff's office from every nook and corner of this town. News stations across the state have already begun to pick them up. Rumors of a chupacabra monster lurking in Boca Falls are about to become front-page news."

I stayed quiet. But my eyes once again involuntarily flicked toward my bedroom. This time, I was afraid Skennyrd might've noticed.

I held my breath. The Incredible Hulk's slightly smaller and significantly less green doppelgänger stared straight at me. His look was sharp enough to slice caña.

I could feel myself shrinking under the penetrating scrutiny of those snakelike eyes, and it was all I could do not to chitter and scurry away like a mouse.

Finally, Skennyrd said, "Well, I think you've been enough help for one night." The entire couch sighed in relief as he rose slowly and started toward the door.

Then, with one catcher's-mitt-size hand swallowing the knob, he turned back to say, "I *am* going to hunt down your little pet, Jorge. And its head *is* going up on my wall."

And with a slam of the door, he was gone.

CHAPTER 32

Skennyrd had been right. Over the next couple of days, more and more eyewitness reports came pouring in by the hour, by the *minute*. They were all over the news. And with all the reports of vamp'd cows, sheep, goats, and chickens, and all the rumored sightings of strange, night-lurking, and potentially *bloodsucking* creatures on the loose, the whole town was loco-ing out.

Now, had it just been Principal Skennyrd hunting Carter, we would've been in hot water. Scalding hot, as a matter of fact. But we might've gotten through it. *Maybe.*

Except it wasn't just Skennyrd...

Thanks to all the news coverage, a slew of trophy hunters had descended on our tiny little New Mexican town like a troop of sugar addicts on a cotton candy machine. Men and women in matching camo jackets and hats, with big guns, bigger trucks, and itchy trigger fingers.

You could see them everywhere, in the fields and woods in the daytime, setting up tents in the grass and hunting saddles high in the trees. And at night, the restless glow of their flashlights lit the woods with an otherworldly brilliance, making them look like some neon bird's nest from another planet.

But as concerning as the hunters were, maybe even *more* concerning—at least to me—were the dips. I mean, what if everything Carter had said about them was true? What if they were as hot on his trail as he thought they were? And what if they really were supernatural?

The net of danger closing in around my best friend felt as wide as the Pacific Ocean, and as inevitable as a final exam.

That was why from the night of Skennyrd's visit, I'd gone into extreme lockdown mode, keeping Carter in my room and out of the crosshairs of anyone's high-powered hunting rifle.

I also decided it was about time we fine-tuned our "smuggle Carter out of Boca Falls" plan. So Liza, Ernie, and I began to make some tweaks to it, accounting for the new variables (aka *hunters*), and Liza even helped me out with the chupachow, smuggling Carter about a gallon of animal blood each day.

But let me just say: housebreaking a chupacabra ain't easy. And keeping him out of sight of a shrewd, nosy, and completely distrusting grandmother is almost impossible!

As the days passed, I could see Carter growing more and more restless. He was like a caged . . . well, *chupacabra*.

He was mad anxious to go outside. To breathe fresh, wild air again. And I really couldn't blame him. I was getting pretty used to the stuff myself.

But since his only options were to hang out in my closet or become a mount on someone's wall, he didn't really give me a hard time.

All there was really left to do now was wait.

CHAPTER 33

Friday, October 31st. Halloween. The day of the big school play, and the day we were going to put Carter on a train that would eventually—*hopefully*—get him out of Boca Falls and reunite him with his family.

The four of us had spent pretty much every waking hour since Skennyrd's little visit going over every last detail of the plan. Every possibility. Every contingency.

So it was no surprise that when the big day finally came, we worked with the kind of down-to-the-second precision that would've made an atomic clock blush.

At 7:08 a.m., Ernie showed up at my house and handed me the one-way train ticket he'd bought for Carter.

At 7:10, I slipped it into the top drawer of my

dresser and told Carter to keep an eye on it through the closet slats.

At 7:11, I reminded him not to come out—*no matter what!*—until I came back to get him.

At 7:31, Ernie and I met up with Liza at school, and she handed me a grocery bag with the backup costume she'd whipped up for Carter. (We'd figured that we'd better have a plan B in case someone realized what he actually was, so we decided to go with my original idea: a humongous white sheet with a pair of eyeholes cut out—aka your classic ghost costume.)

At 7:33, the costume was stuffed into the big pocket of my bookbag.

At 7:39, Ernie called his mom to remind her that after the play, she had to take us and "a friend" (ahem, *a seven-foot-tall bloodsucker*) trick-or-treating in the Las Joyas neighborhood, which—surprise, surprise—just so happened to be a mere five-minute walk from the train station.

At 7:45, Liza called her dad and gave him the same spiel; that way, if anything happened to go wrong with Ernie's mom's SUV, like a flat tire or something, we'd have an alternate pair of wheels at the ready.

At 12:01 p.m., just after lunch, the three of us made

our way to the rear of the main auditorium along with the rest of the sixth grade to get ready for the play.

And by 3:00, the props were set, the lighting was perfect, and the parents and locals were already streaming in.

The play would begin at 3:45 sharpish, it would end at 5:15 sharpish, and then we'd be sharpishly on our way back to my house to pick up Carter.

That was the plan.

And up until exactly 5:00, everything went exactly according *to* that plan.

But then, well—I guess you could say things got a little hairy.

And I mean that in the furriest sense possible . . .

Our very hairy situation

CHAPTER 34

It was the closing minute of the closing act. The moment when Kim Reynolds, the student playing the chupacabra (the one who me, Liza, and Ernie made the costume for) was supposed to wander out onstage and do some silly skit that would close the show.

Except that Liza, Ernie, and I were all backstage, and Kim was still backstage with us. Still waiting for her cue. And *still* in costume.

Which meant that the chupacabra onstage *wasn't* Kim, and *wasn't* wearing a costume. At least not the one we made.

Exactly fifty-six seconds ago, the entire auditorium had been pitch-dark while the prop teams did their thing, dragging out all the cardboard bushes and cardboard trees that were supposed to resemble a big, wide-open forest.

But as the lights slowly brightened, and my eyes gradually adjusted to the glare of the overhead spotlights, I did a double take. No, a triple take!

Because the giant Chewbacca look-alike that had climbed up onstage was none other than my best friend. It was *Carter*!

Eyes bugging, I looked at Ernie, and he looked at Liza, and she looked at Carter, who looked around the dark "woods" with the corners of his furry, fang-lined mouth pinched with concern.

I heard Kim angrily whisper, "Who is *that*?"

Then, just like the script called for, our school mascot, Billy the billy goat, made his grand appearance. Whoever was unlucky enough to be inside the big goat costume came "galloping" and "bleating" from the other side of the stage.

And the moment he did, I saw the chupacabra's mismatched eyes flash.

Then I saw them narrow. Narrow hungrily.

And narrow on Billy.

Uh-oh.

CHAPTER 35

In a blink, the chupacabra leapt clear across the stage as if hooked up to a fly-wire system, and—

SLAM!

He tackled the oblivious chivo like he thought it was dinner! To be fair, for Carter, goat usually *was* dinner...

Billy the billy goat screeched and kicked. The audience gasped. Carter hissed. His razor-sharp claws sank deep into the fuzzy, rumpled haunches of the mascot costume, and his gleaming white fangs sank even deeper into the plushy gray neck.

My heart stopped.

Time stopped.

Billy stopped.

Everything just *stopped*!

I had time to think, *He killed him . . . He killed BILLY!*

But as the kangaroo-like head of the chupacabra slowly lifted, and his eyes gazed dazedly around the dark auditorium, I saw that there was no blood on his fangs, or on the tips of his claws, or anywhere on the bulky, cottony carcass of the wannabe caprine.

In other words, Carter hadn't killed anything!

I watched the chupacabra stare quizzically out at the people in the audience, as if he'd just noticed them for the first time.

Then all of a sudden, he stiffened. His curly fur bristled. He wheezed and hiccupped, and burped and hissed, arching his back and bracing himself two-handedly against the stage floor like some overgrown house cat preparing to cough up the world's gnarliest hair ball.

Then he *did* cough up the world's gnarliest hair ball!

A slimy grayish knot about the size of a youth soccer ball (and clearly made of Billy's cottony/

polyester innards) landed wetly on the stage.

For a moment no one moved.

No one even *breathed*.

I half expected the audience members to leap out of their seats, taking up pitchforks and torches as they charged the stage shouting, "*¡MONSTRUO! KILL IT!*"

But then . . . a laugh bubbled up out of the crowd.

There came a second.

And then a third.

Somebody somewhere began a slow clap and was slowly joined by someone else . . . and the next thing I knew, the entire auditorium erupted into laughter and applause!

They think this is all some kind of joke, I realized. *That it's part of the play!*

A moment later, Billy staggered unsteadily to his feet and limped off toward the exit.

A moment after that, the final curtain dropped.

And a moment after *that*, I rushed out onstage, grabbing Carter by the arm and hissing, "*Dude, what are you doing here?*"

"I followed your scent," the chupacabra explained, wiggling his muzzle-y nose. "It was easy, too. You should try to be a little less nervous, ¿sabes? Your hormones totally givin' you away."

"Forget my hormones!" I snapped. "I don't care how you got here—I want to know *why* you got here! ¿Estás loco, o qué?"

"It's the hunter . . ." he said ominously. "He *huntin'* me!"

CHAPTER 36

Ernie and Liza joined us center stage.

Ernie said, "The hunter?"

And Liza said, "You mean Skennyrd?"

Carter's skinny shoulders went up and down like he wasn't sure. "It was the same chupadedo came over to la casa with Jorge's sneaker!"

"That was *Skennyrd*!" I rasped, hardly believing my ears. "So he found you at my house?"

And even before Carter could nod, it hit me. The night Skennyrd had come over! I'd accidentally glanced toward my bedroom when he was interrogating me! When he was asking about the "creature." He must've noticed. I'd given us away!

"I heard a window break after your grandparents left for the store," Carter said. "Then he found me in your room an' tried to *shoot* me!"

Liza gulped. Ernie gaped. I did a bit of both, feeling my panic-o-meter spike through the *ROOF*!

"Please tell me you brought the train ticket," I said to Carter, and my insides twisted as the chupacabra's shoulders dropped and he shook his furry head.

"¡No tuve oportunidad!" he said mournfully.

I squeezed my eyes shut. Guess you could say we were in quite the pickle. Which really sucked because I hated pickles! Especially those really itty-bitty sour ones they serve in delis.

Behind me, someone said, "Hey, what gives?" It was Kim. She was still in her chupacabra costume.

Kim gave me a dry stare. *Desert* dry.

"*Another chupacabra . . . ?*" whispered Carter, sounding and looking completamente shocked. His blue eye had grown to the size of a beach ball, and his green one stared back at Kim like she'd just hatched from a giant dinosaur egg.

"That's what I'm saying!" shouted Kim.

"Hey, uh . . ." I gave Liza and Ernie the please-escort-you-know-who-off-the-premises look, and they quickly got the message.

As they half talked, half dragged Kim off the stage, Carter said excitedly, "Who was dat?"

"Kim," I answered, barely paying him any attention. I was too busy trying to figure out our next move.

"Kim?" he repeated. "¡Órale! Does she live in the woods nearby?"

"*No!*" I snapped. "She lives in a *house*. Kim's a student here!"

THEY LET CHUPACABRAS GO TO SCHOOL HERE?!

"Dude, forget Kim!" I shouted. "She's not into chupacabras, okay?"

A bunch of people laughed. Someone made a loud snorting sound. Far away, a baby giggled.

And *that's* when I realized a few very important things.

One, the stage curtain had gone back up. A *while* ago.

Two, most of the audience was still in their seats, eyes glued to the stage.

And three, at the other end of the stage, standing there like some jacket-wearing mountain with a long black hunting rifle gripped firmly in his huge pale hands, was Principal Skennyrd.

CHAPTER 37

"*RUN!*" I screamed, shoving Carter. Then I grabbed the nearest "tree" and flung it at Elmer Fudd's gigantic cousin.

I'm not sure what happened next. All I know is that there was this huge *BOOM!* and the tree exploded like a piñata made of papier-mâché. The audience members laughed and cheered, stomping their feet, as Carter and I shrieked and hauled nachas out of there.

Outside, we didn't waste any time. Carter summoned his inner Shadowfax while I summoned my inner Gandalf, and after I hopped on his back, we rode like the wind!

From that point on, it was a flat-out race back to my house, and the moment we got to the front door, the first thing I did was dig the huge white bedsheet/ghost costume out of my bookbag and drape it over Carter.

Once I got the eyeholes lined up (well, more or less), we ran straight inside as I shouted, "Grandma! Grandma! Where are you?"

"What now?" she called from the kitchen.

We found her hanging out at the breakfast nook, stuffing her face with fun-size Snickers bars and casually tossing the empty wrappers into a bowl with a Post-it note that read: TAKE AS MANY AS YOU'D LIKE. HAPPY HALLOWEEN!

For some reason, that stopped me. "Uh, what are you doing?" I couldn't help but ask.

"It's trick-or-treat day, no? Well, anyone who stops by this house is getting tricked, 'cause granny's eating all the treats. Wacha!"

Ugh. The house was sooo going to get egged. "Listen, I need a huge favor!" I said desperately.

With a mouthful of milk chocolate, roasted peanuts, and creamy nougat, she replied, "You're in my light."

And okay, I'll admit it—at that point, I pretty much *lost it.* I mean, we didn't have time for this!

"It isn't *your* light!" I burst out. "It's GOD'S light! It's EVERYONE'S light! It's freakin' *SUNSHINE!*"

Sighing, Paz tossed another empty wrapper into the bowl. "What do you want?"

"Please drive me and my friend to Las Joyas. We want to go trick-or-treating."

"No."

"But *why not?*"

"Because I said so. That's whhhyyyy, Mr. Whiny Pants. You need to toughen up, kid. And why you crying, huh?"

"I'm not crying!" I snapped. "My eyes just mist sometimes when I get angry! There's a BIG difference!" Man, this lady was *impossible!* "Anyway, Las Joyas is right around the corner! It's not like I'm asking you to drive us to Disney World."

"I don't know what it's not, but I'll tell you what it is: *you're a liar.* And I don't drive liars *any*where. Not to Disney World, and not even to la esquina!" Her eyes flicked to Carter. "Wow, you must've had one heck of a growth spurt, huh, Ernie?"

Carter only nodded. I gave him a mental high five. He'd obviously been studying "the rules."

"What are you even talking about?" I said to Paz. "What have I lied about?"

"For one, you conveniently forgot to mention that you've had a *chupacabra* living under my roof for the past week!"

Now, that *really* stopped me. It was one of those total flan-to-the-face moments. Carter looked pretty shocked, too. Well, as shocked as you can look through a bedsheet.

"How—how'd you know?" I whispered.

"I might've been born late," my grandma said, "but I wasn't born *clueless.* Remember, I've lived on this farm for over sesenta años—that's *sixty years.* You don't think in all that time a chupacabra never passed through here? Plus, I saw the giant fang marks on my boxes of red wine."

"Grandma, listen," I said. "They're not like everyone thinks! They're *not* monsters!"

"I know that!" she shot back. "I told you, I've known chupacabras since before you were even a twinkle in your father's lazy eye!"

I blinked. "My father has a lazy eye?"

"Yeah, and lazy arms and lazy legs, too. That's why he could never hold down a job. But my point is,

I know all about chupacabras. Heck, my best friend growing up, Chalupa, she was a chupacabra!"

"Oh, I know her!" Carter suddenly piped up. He swung his eyes around to me, nodding his sheet-draped head excitedly like, *It's true!* "Chalupa's one of the best chupacabra chefs ever!"

"That's right," agreed Paz, turning to me. "Who do you think gave Taco Bell their nacho cheese chalupa recipe?"

For what felt like a long time, all I could do was gape at her.

My grandma knew about Carter.

My grandma had known other chupacabras. I could hardly wrap my brain around it. But hey, at least it was better than a total *loco-out*.

Finally, I managed, "Well, we need to get *this* chupacabra out of Boca Falls. And *fast*! Hunters are crawling all over town, and the principal from my school is pretty set on turning him into office décor. Will you help us?"

My abuela popped another bite-size Snickers into her mouth. "Sure, I'll help. But for a price."

"A *price*? What price?"

"Tomorrow you're on chicken-plucking duty."

"*Chicken-plucking duty*? Grandma, are you seriously going to try to negotiate with me when there's a living thing's *LIFE* on the line?"

"This ain't a negotiation," Paz said. "It's a take-it-or-leave-it."

Shaking my head, I let out a huge annoyed groan. You know, just so she understood how I felt about her taking advantage of the situation—and me—like this.

Man, the things you do for amigos.

"In that case, I'll take it," I said.

"Great choice!" Carter agreed.

Then I ran off to grab the giant furball's train ticket.

CHAPTER 38

If someone had come up with a list of the biggest surprises I'd have that day, my grandma knowing about the existence of chupacabras would have been right at the top of that list.

I mean, at the very tippy-top. But as it turned out, it wasn't even the biggest surprise of the next *sixty seconds*.

Because instead of grabbing the truck keys and heading out the front door, Paz grabbed another set of keys—hidden in el gabinete—and led us out the back to the busted-looking barn behind the chicken coop, the one with a big King Kong–size lock on its crusty, clunky doors.

And the second those doors were rolled open, my eyeballs nearly rolled out of *my face*!

Because chilling in that gross old barn was something I'd never expected.

Keying the ignition, she flipped a few switches and the hot pink carrucha did the lowrider shimmy, hopping and jumping and dancing all over the place.

As we climbed into the back, Carter looked like he was on the verge of a heart attack. Me, on the other hand, I was just laughing my *butt* off.

Then my abuela hit the radio. And guess what song came blasting out of the speakers? The ultimate lowrider anthem, "Low Rider" by War, performed by Carlos Santana!

"Hold on to your sombreros, muchachos!" shouted my abuela.

CHAPTER 39

In case you're wondering, it's true what the song says. Lowriders really *are* just "a little higher." It's not something you can exactly put your finger on. But cruising around in one somehow makes the sky seem a little bluer, the grass a little greener, and the whole wide world just a little bit brighter. You mix that with Malo jamming out on the radio and the fresh autumn air blowing in your hair, and you could see why lowrider culture was so popular.

I could have happily cruised down that dusty backcountry road forever.

Unfortunately, we barely made it another half a mile before things took a sharp detour into No Buenosville.

We were getting ready to make a right onto the main road when—

CRASH!

Metal screeched. A rear tire exploded. The low-rider wobbled and lurched, lurched and wobbled.

Then we spun out, half on the road, half in the woods, with my heart half in my throat and half in my toes.

Someone had hit us. Or more like *rammed* us!

And in the rearview mirror, all I saw was *trouble*.

1) "Note the murderous glare in his eyes"

2) "Observe the white-knuckled grip on the steering wheel"

3) "Check out the terrifying array of high-powered hunting rifles"

Yep, this was definitely No Buenosville. Population: Us

"*¡CORRAN!*" my abuela screamed. "I'll slow him down as long as I can!"

She didn't need to tell us twice. Scrambling out of the Chevy, we plunged headfirst into the woods.

Storm clouds were rolling in overhead. The wind shrieked. Branches whipped at our faces and scratched at our arms as we dashed between the trees.

We ran until my sides ached, and my lungs burned, and my sneakers got all scratched up and dirty, and leaves stuck to my cheeks. Then the clouds burst, tearing open with gashes of angry lightning.

Rain began to pour down in sheets. In buckets. Puddles swelled up all around us, among the ditches and roots, and we were instantly drenched to the bone.

Carter's ghost costume was plastered to his fur like a saggy, semitransparent second skin. He stopped running. So I stopped running, too. I stared up at him and he stared down at me.

"Don't say it," I whispered. "*¡Vamos!* Let's keep going!"

But the chupacabra shook his head. His pointy ears were twitching anxiously. "He's huntin' me. Not you."

"No. See, *you're* my best friend, and if anyone's got

a problem with *you*, they've got a problem with me! I'm not leaving you until you're on that train."

"Jorge, you *have* to go back."

"No!"

"Yes! These woods full of hunters! If they see me, they gonna shoot. And if they miss, they maybe hit *you*. Y eso no es algo que yo puedo de—"

Suddenly, from somewhere in the trees came a thunderous *CRACK!*

Then several things happened at once. Something small and silvery came hissing through the rain-soaked air. It whispered past my face and over my shoulder, and then through the thin, cottony fabric of Carter's ghost costume, down by his knee. A spot of blood blossomed there, bright red against the crisp white of the bedsheet.

I watched the chupacabra's eyes go wide, I watched his arms drop, I watched his mouth fall open like he was about to say something; but for several seconds, he only stood there, looking at me with an expression like, *What just happened?*

Then his skinny legs buckled, and he dropped flat on his side, splashing the muddy ground as he collapsed.

Terror squeezed my heart like an iron fist. "*Carter!*" I screamed, dropping down next to him.

And an instant later, an enormous figure emerged from the trees and pouring rain.

Skennyrd.

His face was a hard, pitiless mask. His gigantic black boots made no noise on the tangled ground as he stalked toward us, one eye sighting down the length of a wicked-looking rifle.

"Back away from the monster," he said, holding the weapon steady. "And don't think I won't put a bullet through your arm to put one in its heart."

"STOP!" I cried. "Just *stop*! He's not a monster! He's not a killer!"

"Don't make me tell you twice, boy," growled Skennyrd.

A sharp metallic *click* rang out as he racked back the slide on the rifle. The sound was like a baseball smacking off a tin roof.

Then I heard another sound. It seemed to be coming from everywhere, all around us—a harsh, threatening snarling that made all the little hairs on the back of my neck instantly stand on end.

In the same moment, a flash of bluish lightning

lit up the world, revealing nothing but endless empty woods as far as the eye could see.

When the lightning flickered again, I saw them.

And as the monsters melted out of the shadows and rain, two thoughts rushed into my brain at the exact same time.

The first was: *Dips! Those must be the awful, blood-sucking, supernatural vampire dogs that Carter told me about!*

The second was even worse: *And we're about to become vampire-doggy biscuits . . .*

CHAPTER 40

Skennyrd had spotted the monsters, too. Only he was trying not to let them know, watching them sneakily from deep inside the pale cinder block of his head.

Then, suddenly, he whipped around, spinning and shooting at the same time.

A bright yellow flash exploded from the muzzle of his rifle as it barked out several fast shots in the direction of the vampire dogs.

A spine-tingling howl erupted from the trees. One of the monstruos shrieked, retreating into the shadows, just as another howled, lunging toward us.

It slammed into Skennyrd's refrigerator-width back—*WHAM!*—and they both disappeared behind a stand of scrubby trees as several more shots rang out. Next thing I knew, I heard the crunch of leaves ...

the crack of branches . . . and I slowly turned, and
even more slowly looked up.

The vampire dog lunged. I fumbled backward.
My foot caught on a fallen branch, and I came down
hard on my butt as el monstruo landed on top of me,
snarling and growling and flashing its deadly teeth.

I dodged, rolling left just as a massive paw raked
the earth, tearing up weeds. Then I tried rolling right,
thinking I might be able to slip out from underneath
it, but the giant evil perro was way too fast!

Bright red pain screamed through me as a paw the size of a manhole cover slammed down in the center of my chest, pinning me to the ground like an insect to a corkboard. I kicked and flailed, struggled and screamed, but it was totally useless.

The dip was unbelievably heavy! And *unimaginably* strong!

All I could do was lie there, squirming, staring helplessly up at its soulless red eyes as its jaws opened and its stinking breath washed hotly over my skin.

Then fangs—¡Dios mío, longer than Edward Scissorhands's fingers!—reached out for me as the monster moved in for the kill.

CHAPTER 41

You know how everyone says that your life flashes before your eyes just before you die? Well, hate to ruin it for you, but it *doesn't*.

At least it didn't for me.

Because the only thing I could see through the rain was a rabid, snarling mouth, and deadly, drool-slicked fangs.

At that point, there was only one thing left to do. I shut my eyes, preparing for the inevitable and hoping very, *very* hard that the vampire dog's teeth wouldn't hurt nearly as bad as they looked like they were going to.

Then came a sudden *WHOOSH!* like some giant had swung an enormous tree-trunk-size baseball bat past my face.

I felt the crushing weight of the dip suddenly lifted. My eyes snapped open just in time to catch a glimpse of Carter plowing into the monstruo with the perfect technique of an NFL linebacker, and they both went rolling along the ground in a blur of claws and flashing fangs.

When they'd stopped, Carter came out on top, but five other vampire dogs sprang out of the trees around us. And as they leapt onto the chupacabra's back, howling and barking, tearing off his ghost costume, he let out an awful, piercing cry!

Scrambling to my feet, I screamed, "*CARTER!*"

Fear tried to freeze me in place. It tried to make me turn around and run away. Run for my life. But I couldn't. I *wouldn't!*

See, I'd never had a best friend before. I'd never met anyone who made me feel like I *belonged* before, like he did. All the years of feeling lonely and different and completely misunderstood had ended the day I'd met that "monster." The day I'd met Carter.

I'd finally found a real friend. Someone who liked me. Someone who *got* me. Someone I could talk to and just be myself around.

That was friendship. That was special.

And now that I'd found it, I wasn't about to lose it. Not like this. And *definitely* not to those things.

Gritting my teeth, I snatched up the longest, thickest, gnarliest-looking branch in sight. Yep, it was finally time to put my baseball skills to real-world use.

But no matter how many vampire dogs I clob-bered, or how hard I clobbered them, the dips kept coming. More and more every second. Or maybe it was just the same ones, and I wasn't really hurting them!

Still, I swung and I swatted while Carter bit and clawed, and we got all muddy and tired, and even-tually wound up back-to-back, panting and looking wildly around for another furry vampire-dog heinie to kick.

Only ... there weren't any.

They were gone.

The dips were *gone*!

Somehow, someway, we'd fought them off!

"Did we ... *win*?" I asked, glancing dazedly around.

"I think so?" Carter didn't sound too sure about it, either.

"But ... *how*?"

"Los ancients!" the chupacabra suddenly shouted. "Remember what they said? They said that the only way to drive away darkness is with a kindness of the soul! Friendship. Love. Sacrifice. So maybe you riskin' yourself to save me, and me riskin' myself to save you—*true friendship*—maybe that's what scared those monstruos off!"

I had a feeling he was right, too. "Dude, I'm just glad we aren't being digested right now!" Honestly? I felt like we'd just won the World Series!

CHAPTER 42

We found Principal Skennyrd a few yards away, pushing slowly to his knees. He was dripping mud and rainwater and bleeding from several deep scratches on his arms.

I don't think he realized it, but Carter and I had pretty much saved his hide by drawing the dips away. Actually, scratch that. I *know* he didn't realize it, because when he saw us coming, he didn't throw himself gratefully at our feet, thanking us and begging our forgiveness in a teary-eyed plea. Nope. In fact, he did pretty much the *opposite* of that. In one super quick move, he unslung his crossbow, leveling it on Carter.

But that wasn't even the worst part.

The worst part was that before I could say anything—even a single word!—Skennyrd fired.

The arrow that had been loaded in the bow's shallow groove sprang into the air, flying straight at us. Straight at Carter!

I didn't think. I just shoved the chupacabra, and even though it hardly moved him, that was enough.

The good news: the arrow whistled past the spiky matted fur of Carter's left arm.

The bad news: it hit my significantly-less-fur-covered one instead.

I cried out as the razor-sharp arrowhead opened a

gash maybe five inches long across my forearm.

Now, mind you, I'd been cut before. *Lots* of times. I'd cut myself with pocketknives and steak knives, with rocks and screwdrivers, with staples, with thumbtacks, and even with the beak of a tiny origami goose. (Don't ask.) But never—not once—had a cut burned as bad as this one. In fact, if I didn't know any better, I would've guessed someone had poured spicy hot jalapeño juice over it!

Beside me, Carter gave a ferocious hiss and called out my name.

Skennyrd, meanwhile, had been fumbling with his crossbow, trying to reload. But before he could notch another arrow, Carter pounced on him, lifting his rhino-size body off the ground as easily as I could lift an action figure, and then—*CLUNK!*—slamming him into a tree trunk and pinning him there.

The claws of Carter's right hand flashed in an arc of lightning as he reared back, getting ready to slash—*to kill!*—and I cried, "CARTER, *NO!*"

The chupacabra hesitated.

But only for a moment.

A wildness shone in his eyes and gleamed in his

fangs and rippled down his back in angry waves.

And suddenly, I knew *exactly* how Fay Wray felt in the original *King Kong*!

Skennyrd—no big surprise—wasn't doing himself any favors. Those beady rattlesnake eyes of his were venomous as ever as he stared defiantly down at the raging chupacabra.

"What are you waiting for, *monster*?" he roared. "I don't fear you! Do what you were born to do—kill! *Kill!*"

Oh my gosh—no!

"Carter, don't listen to him!" I pleaded, my voice breaking. My heart breaking, too. Hot tears were already burning down my cheeks, but I knew they wouldn't be enough to stop him. Not even close. I didn't quit, though. I screamed, "Carter, you're not un monstruo! You . . . you're more human than anyone I've ever met!"

It was the truth, too. See, in my opinion, being human really came down to having a heart. Not a literal, physical heart (every Tom, Dick, and Bailey had one of those), but a metaphoric one. It came down to having compassion for those around you. Caring as much about other people as you care about yourself. And Carter had that. He had it like a stray dog has fleas. Still, did I seriously think me pouring my soul out to the guy in the middle of a thunderstorm was going to stop him from turning Skennyrd into a side of pee-pee-flavored bacon bits? No. Because this wasn't some corny, made-for-TV movie. Yet, somehow, someway, it *did* . . .

The chupacabra blinked. The hundred muscles of his lanky arms relaxed, then, all at once, the rage in his eyes and in his face began to drain away. Slowly, slowly at first, and then all together, like an unclogging sink.

He let Skennyrd go, and the big coward hit the

ground running—literally—stampeding off into the trees like the first elephant to ever meet a mouse. So much for the Mr. Tough Guy act, huh?

The chupacabra's blue eye found mine first. Next came his green one. There was shock in them. And confusion.

But then, like a ray of early morning sunshine bursting through a bank of dark clouds, his familiar fangy smile began to creep slowly across his fangy face until he practically glowed with it.

"I'm not a monster . . ." he whispered. "I've never *been* a monster. So I don't have to act like one."

"That's right!" I said. "It doesn't matter how people see us. It only matters how we see ourselves!"

Looked like we'd both had enough of living up to people's twisted expectations. Yay us!

I'd just started toward the big ole furball, beaming like a big *goof* ball, when a hot flash of pain lit up my arm.

I gasped, clapping a hand over the arrow wound as another painful stab shot up toward my elbow, underneath the skin.

Carter's gaze flew anxiously around. Lunging, he retrieved Skennyrd's arrow, which had buried itself into the trunk of a nearby tree, and sniffed the silver head.

Suddenly, his dark eyes filled with even darker fear.

"Poison flecha," he breathed. I saw the wet fur of his arms go spiky with dread, and I thought, *Oh, snap! That's right!*

It was Skennyrd's lucky arrow. The one he'd coated with *rattlesnake* poison!

"You go!" I told Carter. "I'll have my grandma take me to the hospital. *Go!*"

But right as I took my next step, the world wobbled, which made me wobble, and Carter had to catch me to keep me from falling down.

"You won't make it," he whispered. He sounded worried. Looked it, too. "El veneno is too strong."

"Estoy bien," I said. "I'm fine!" But the truth was, I wasn't so sure. My eyelids had begun to feel as if someone had hung ten-pound dumbbells from my lashes.

I murmured something. It might've been "Just go."

But Carter said no. Then he said, "There's only one way."

I watched the chupacabra's mouth open wide, like a yawning lion, and his fangs seemed to stretch.

Wait. That wasn't right. His fangs *literally* stretched. Lengthening out of his gums like Wolverine's claws right before a rumble. It was the raddest, most terrifying thing I'd ever seen!

"I have to suck da poison out," he said. "Won't hurt. Think mosquito bite."

"Dude, *no!*" I shouted. "You're waaaay bigger than any mosquito! Plus, I can't even handle needles, and you're going to use *fangs!*"

"It's the only way," Carter whispered. "La única manera."

"At least tell me you've already had breakfast!" I shrieked, half kidding, half not.

"No time for jokes, Jorge."

He was right, too. I could already feel my strength fading fast. Could feel the hot sting of the poison scorching its way through my veins. So I didn't argue.

I just closed my eyes, waiting for the chupacabra to sink his teeth into me.

Honestly, I didn't even want to think about how much this was going to hurt. Once, when I was seven, I'd fallen off my bike and broken my collarbone. All I remembered about the pain was that it had felt *ginormous*. Like it had become my entire world. This probably wasn't going to hurt any less. I mean, how could it? So I braced myself, squeezing my fists and gritting my teeth and getting ready to cry out in utter, bitter agony as those massive, curved fangs—

"All done," Carter said.

Say what?

Wasn't that much poison. By the way, did I mention chupacabras are immune to snake venom?

Gaping, shaking my head, I glanced down at my arm. And yep, there they were—two fang-like marks on either side of the arrowhead gash.

Funny part was, they weren't even bleeding! And neither was the gash. In fact, all the skin in that area looked like it had already begun to seal up!

"Chupacabra saliva also got some intense healing properties," Carter explained. He grinned wildly, with about as many teeth as a great white shark. "Pretty chido, huh?"

"Yeah." I grinned back. "Pretty awesome."

CHAPTER 43

We arrived at the train station just as the final boarding call rang out over the PA system. Ernie and Liza were pacing anxiously by the gate. When they spotted us, they rushed over, and Ernie handed Carter a Captain Kirk lunch box. "Just a snack," he said. "In case you get hungry."

"Hurry!" Liza said. "Everyone's boarding!"

All around us, zombies and martians were climbing onto the train, while Wonder Women and X-Men waved at witches and werewolves from the windows.

I blinked up at Carter. My insides were moving the way they did when it was my turn up to bat in Little League. The way they always did on a full count.

I said, "You know the way to Calle Hueso, right?"

Carter nodded. "I know the way."

"And you've got the train ticket?"

Carter nodded again. "I got the ticket."

"And your list of rules?"

"Got that, too."

I held my breath. A sparkling rainbow of emotions was passing through me. I could feel every single color, the entire spectrum. I felt scared and proud, and nervous and happy, and anxious, and calm, and sad, and I felt it all at once.

Now I know how moms and dads feel dropping their kids off for their first day at kindergarten, I thought, and I tried not to cry, even though everything in me wanted to.

My voice broke as I whispered, "I . . . I'm not too good at goodbyes."

"I'm not too good at them, either."

"Will you ever come back to Boca Falls?"

"I hope so."

"I hope so, too."

Carter looked down at his new lunch box for a second, and when he looked up again, his mismatched eyes were shiny with tears.

A lump the size of Mount Baldy had formed in

my throat. I bit my lower lip, but it wasn't enough to stop the tears.

"Don't cry, Jorge," Carter whispered. "Goodbye's not forever. But good friends are."

"I hope you find your family," I said.

"And I hope you get to go back home."

With a wobbly smile, I wiped my cheeks. Then I looked slowly around at Liza and Ernie, and up at Carter, too, and said, "Thanks, but, uh, actually I think I might hang out in New Mexico for a while. I met some pretty cool peeps down here. Besides, home is a feeling, right?"

A slow, happy grin spread across the chupacabra's furry lips. "Home is a feeling," he agreed.

Just then, a high-pitched whistle split the air— that sad and lonely sound of departure.

"All aboard!" a voice blared over the PA system.

There was nothing left to say. So I just hugged my best friend and he hugged me back. Liza and Ernie hugged Carter, too. And even after all the hugs were exchanged and Carter disappeared onto the train through a door that barely fit him, and the train began chugging along, pulling slowly away from the station, I just stood there, watching it go.

"Man, I'm happy for him," Ernie said after a few seconds. "And I know how dangerous things were getting and everything—but did he really have to leave? I mean, I thought he kinda loved us . . ."

"Just because someone leaves doesn't mean they don't love you," I said. "Sometimes people leave *because* they love you. Carter taught me that."

The last few train cars were already melting into the hazy horizon as Liza hooked an arm through mine. Giving me a squeeze, she said, "Something tells me we're going to see him again."

And that made me smile.

Even through the tears.

ACKNOWLEDGMENTS

Publishing a book is most definitely a team sport. So here's a huge and heartfelt THANK YOU! to all our wonderful teammates at Viking Children's Books, who helped turn this book from a dream to reality.

To our amazing and über-talented editor, Jenny Bak—thank you so much for all your wisdom, support, and sleepless nights! To Ken Wright, our publisher—thank you for believing in *ChupaCarter*!

To the world's greatest illustrator, Santy Gutiérrez—thank you for bringing the characters out of our imaginations and making them even cooler! To Opal Roengchai, our amazing cover and interior designer—thank you for an awesome cover and a killer layout!

Big, big thanks to Gaby Corzo, Krista Ahlberg, Sola Akinlana, Abigail Powers, Marinda Valenti,

Kelley Salas, Delia Davis, Vanessa Robles, and the fantastic Jennifer Dee and Elyse Marshall. You all rock!

And last but by no means least, to superstar agents extraordinaire Albert Lee from United Talent Agency and Rena Rossner from the Deborah Harris Agency—thank you both for everything!

LOOK FOR THE NEXT

ADVENTURE!